Tempting the Billionaire

A Boston Billionaires Book

Penelope Ryan

D1736360

Emma: It started as the only way out of an impossible situation. Seduce the billionaire, and my ex won't share private videos of me. But Ezra is more than just the heir to a billion-dollar empire. And the way he makes me feel, the dirty things he does to me—now that I've gotten a taste, I don't know if I can live without it.

Ezra: I've never felt this way about a woman before, and despite the possibility for scandal, I can't keep my thoughts off of her—or my hands. Emma just might undo me, but I'm willing to risk it all for her.

After leaving her toxic relationship, Emma Hayes is ready to start her life over, rebuild, and heal. And when she lands a job at Bishop Jewelers, the oldest and most prominent seller of fine jewelry on the East Coast, things are looking up. But when Emma's ex learns of her proximity to the company that put his family's store out of business, he's scheming for payback. And Emma is his way in. Threatening to expose private videos of her if she doesn't comply, Emma is suddenly thrown into the middle of a family feud she has no way of solving. Her only way out? Seduce the married heir to Bishop Jewelers, Ezra Bishop, causing a scandal the prominent engagement ring company can never come back from.

From the outside looking in, Ezra Bishop has it all. A beautiful wife, a successful company, and more money than he could ever spend. But he harbors a secret that could ruin him—if it hasn't already ruined his heart. And then along comes Emma Hayes. A gorgeous ray of sunshine that just might save his life—or completely destroy it.

Tropes: age gap, hurt her and I'll kill you, protective alpha male, office romance

HEA guaranteed, no cheating!

Chapter 1

Emma

I drop the final box in the middle of the living room and heave a deep sigh. I glance around at the sea of cardboard, blank walls, and sterile floors. I'm home.

My new home. The home that's going to be a whole lot better than my last one.

While others might see my abrupt turn in life as a step down—newly single, living on my own, in a much smaller and crappier apartment—I see it for what it truly is. Freedom.

It took me far too long to see my relationship with Justin for what it was. Toxic. Borderline verbally abusive. And a hundred percent bad for my mental state. We'd met in college, moved in together right after graduation, and lived together for three years. I've never really known adulthood without him. But while I truly did love him, our relationship was peppered with a dynamic that left me feeling unloved, used, and lonely. And finally, I couldn't take it anymore.

I'd left. The fight was epic, unbearable. I was almost afraid. But ultimately, he'd let me go. And here I am, in my very own apartment, out on my own.

It's strange. I feel eighteen again, going off on my own. But deep down, I know it's good for me.

I reach for the box labeled, "kitchen," pulling out my coffee machine and setting it up for the morning. If there's one thing I need up and running, it's my coffee maker. And I need to be on my best game tomorrow. Because not only have I changed homes, I've changed jobs.

Ever since graduation, I've worked for Justin's family jewelry company. They were hiring, I had an in, and I took a job that I assumed would be temporary that just ended up turning into years. I handled inventory, dealt with customers, and did a lot of the backend administrative work.

That is, until they went out of business three months ago. As a small family company, they just couldn't compete with the big-name jewelers. It was sad—I did truly like Justin's family, and the store—but even if it hadn't gone out of business, I would've left. I need all ties from Justin completely gone from my life.

I shake my head, knowing his blood would boil if he knew the new job I'd picked up. But my only job experience has been working at a jewelry store—it just made sense that that's where I'd apply.

I didn't think I'd immediately be hired by Bishop Jewelers, the oldest and most high-end jeweler on the East Coast. And Justin's family business' rivals for years.

Either way, I'm excited for a fresh start.

I glance around the apartment again, slightly daunted by the amount of boxes. Resigned to simply relax and leave the mess for slightly later, I order some Thai food on my phone. Unpacking can wait for tomorrow evening. Tonight, I plan on eating a delicious Pad Thai and watching reality TV on my laptop.

■■

I stroll down Newbury Street, my kitten heels clacking on the pavement. The street is lined with some of Boston's nicest and fanciest storefronts, including Bishop Jewelers. Nervous butterflies flutter in my stomach. It's a mixture of excitement and anxiety. Excitement because this is a start to my brand-new life. And nerves because I feel like so much is riding on this.

I haven't started a new job in years. And I really want to prove myself. Hence the stiff, high-necked blouse, pencil skirt, and heels. While I'd always dressed nicely at Stoll Jewelry, I never dressed *this* nice. I don't know, something about the high stakes, the Bishop legacy, and the idea of working on Newbury street just got to me, and I'd gone out to buy a completely new wardrobe. Hopefully it pays off.

The shop comes into view, and the butterflies intensify. I take a deep breath before gently pushing the door open and stepping into the grand and beautifully decorated flagship location of Bishop Jewelers. Gorgeous jewelry is displayed beneath elegant glass cases all throughout the store, the warm light above only highlighting their beauty.

"Welcome in," a kind voice calls.

I glance over to see a woman who looks to be about my age smiling at me from behind the counter. "Hi," I say. "My name is Emma Hayes. I'm the new sales associate."

The woman's smile brightens further. "Oh yes, Emma! I was told you'd be in today." She comes around the counter, her hand outstretched. "I'm Rachel."

I shake her hand, feeling a bit of my nerves washing away.

"I'm so glad to finally have another sales associate. There's only a handful of us, meaning I end up working some days here all by myself. It's gets hella boring and lonely."

I laugh. "Glad to be of help."

"I'll show you around," she says, turning and heading back behind the counter. I follow. "The register is over here, along with keys and security system info." Rachel points out all the important aspects of the register, as well as how to turn the security system on when leaving, how to unlock cases, and the like. "I know I'm bombarding you with information, so feel free to re-ask any and all questions later," she says with a laugh. "Also, Ezra will be in later, so you can also ask him questions."

"Ezra?" I ask. I wrack my brain, suddenly panicking that I've forgotten someone important. The person I'd interviewed with was named Beth, the sales manager. Who's Ezra?

"Ezra Bishop," Rachel says. "The heir and current owner of Bishop Jewelers. He runs everything since his father retired about five years ago."

"Oh," I say, feeling slightly embarrassed to not have known. Honestly, I didn't even realize Bishop Jewelers was still family owned and operated. I thought, like the majority of companies, that their name was just a name. Especially for a company as prominent as this.

"How much do you know about jewelry?" she asks me.

"Quite a bit, actually," I say with a humble shrug. "I worked at a jeweler for the last three years."

Rachel's eyes widen in pleasant surprise. "Oh great, then this transition should be a breeze. You know all the basics—gemstones, metals, cut, clarity?"

I nod. "Yep. Could recite it all in my sleep."

She mimes thanking God, rolling her eyes heavenward. I laugh. We spend the next few hours going over various things around the store, stopping to greet customers and help them with questions and sales. I can already feel myself relaxing—I think I'm going to fit in just fine here. Rachel is as nice as can be, and the basics of being a sales associate at a jewelry store are all the same.

I hear the light ring of the bell above the door and look up to see that someone new has entered the store. I move to greet them but am stopped in my tracks when I fully register what is in front of me.

Quite possibly the most attractive man I have ever seen. Tall, lean, speckles of gray in his dark brown hair, wearing a dark blue suit, he strides across the store like he owns it. I resist the urge to physically bite my lip. Holy shit is this guy hot. Probably coming in to buy his lucky lady something special—like most of the men who come in here. Damn, I wish I had someone like this buying me jewelry.

With a physical shake of my head, I snap myself out of it. *Focus, Emma.*

"Welcome to Bishop Jewelers," I call as he approaches the counter, his steps seeming more and more purposeful the closer he gets. "I'm—"

"Emma Hayes," he interrupts me.

I halt, my mouth still open. I blink, then respond, "Yes ..."

The man offers me a small smile, the corners of his eyes crinkling in a way I never thought could be so downright *sexy.* "I'm Ezra Bishop. I was told you'd be starting today." He holds out a hand, and I gingerly take it. His grip is strong and firm, and then it's gone.

"Oh yes," I say, realization dawning on me. Damn, Rachel forgot to mention that Ezra Bishop was the fucking hottest man on the planet. "Mr. Bishop, so nice to meet you."

He shakes his head, coming around the side of the counter and beckoning me to follow him into the back room. "Call me Ezra—Mr. Bishop makes me feel old."

I follow him through a doorway and into a back area I haven't been in yet since Rachel and I have been so busy with customers this morning. There are shelves filled with stock items, along with a workbench where

I assume jewelry is made or repaired. Probably mostly repaired as I assume most of the inventory comes from offsite. Through another doorway, I see a desk and monitor set up. That's where Ezra leads us.

I follow him into the office and take a seat when he gestures to the chair in front of the desk. He sits across from me, booting up his computer.

"So, Beth tells me you've worked in jewelry sales before," he says without looking at me, focused on his computer.

I straighten in my chair. "Yes, I worked at Stoll Jewelry, a small jewelry store downtown, for three years."

He nods. "Great. That's perfect. Should be a breeze picking everything up, then."

"Yeah, and Rachel's been showing me around all morning," I add.

He nods again, finally finishing up on his computer and then turning his attention toward me. His eyes are dark and piercing, and I feel myself shifting uncomfortably in my seat. Although whether from intimidation or something else, I'm not entirely sure.

"Did she tell you about the custom design services we offer?" he asks.

I shake my head, remembering the workbench I'd seen in the corner of the back room.

"So, we offer custom designs—most often we see those on engagement rings. Rachel can outline the pricing structure for you, but it's an important service we offer, so I wanted to make sure you're aware of it. We have an in-house designer, and sometimes I do the designs as well."

"You?" I repeat.

At this, he smirks. "Yes. I could outsource it all, obviously, but I still like to get my hands dirty from time to time, so to speak."

I momentarily fixate on *hands dirty*, but then I chide myself and try to pay attention. "That's ... impressive," I reply.

He shrugs. "It's really not that hard, especially if you practically grew up in this store." He gestures around and then laughs, those adorable crinkles returning to the corners of his eyes.

I smile.

He returns to his computer, clicking away. "Did Beth email you the new hire paperwork?" he asks.

I nod. "Yep, filled it all out last night."

"Great. Well, then you're all set. I think you're going to fit in well here, Emma." He shoots me a warm smile that makes me practically weak in the knees.

Damn, I need to get it together. I can't be crushing on my boss. *Just ignore how hot he is, Emma*, I order myself.

He gestures to the door. "Just shadow Rachel for the rest of the day. And feel free to ask me any questions. I'll be in my office all day."

I stand quickly, uttering an awkward thanks before heading back out to the floor. Rachel is busy ringing up a customer, and when she's done, she hurries over to me.

I shoot her a look. "You forgot to mention that our boss is practically an Abercrombie model," I say under my breath.

She laughs out loud, throwing her head back. "Yeah, I thought it would be funnier to just watch you take it in all at once."

I snort.

"There are worse things than having eye candy for a boss," she murmurs, and I laugh along with her. And I'm sure she's right. There *are* worse things. Although focusing on the job might be just a tad more difficult than I'd imagined.

Chapter 2

Ezra

The heavy door to my Beacon Hill townhouse slams behind me, echoing in the empty space. I walk across the foyer, grabbing a sparkling water from the fridge and then sinking into an armchair in the living room.

A familiar depressing aura settles around me as I sip my water. I've only made the switch to drinking these recently. When I realized that coming home and fixing myself more than a few mixed drinks every night was getting out of hand, I decided I needed to stop myself. So I guess a cran-raspberry fizzy water will have to do.

I sigh, setting the can down on the side table next to me.

A shape out of the corner of my eye catches my attention, and for a split second, I think it's Diane. Even as I turn to see my coat hanging on the coat rack, I know it isn't her.

She moved out two months ago and hasn't been back since. You'd think I'd be used to the empty apartment by now, but it feels as if the nights are just getting longer and longer.

Something needs to change. I just don't know what.

I guess I'm still in shock. In shock that after eight years of marriage, Diane had decided to throw it all away for some guy she worked with. She said that I'd driven her to it. That my long days of work had left her lonely and miserable. And while I'm the first to admit that I can be a bit of a workaholic at times, I still don't think that it excuses cheating.

I'd tried to reason with her, told her we could work things out—that therapy could help us. But I think we both knew that our relationship had run its course. Besides, she was in love with someone else— she *is* in love with some else.

A pit forms in my stomach at the thought of it.

Fuck.

I need to move on. Part of me thinks some kind of rebound might be the best course of action, but then I push the thought away.

Diane and I haven't announced our divorce yet. Even while she's completely moved in with another man, leaving me high and dry, the divorce isn't finalized, and we have yet to come up with a cohesive way to announce our separation.

Boston might be this big cosmopolitan city, but in many ways, it's like a small town. And people love to talk—especially about its elite families, the Bishops being one of them. Especially the family that made its fortune selling engagement rings—our divorce won't exactly go over well. Not that it would be ruinous or anything like that, but I still dread the thought.

I remember when I'd proposed to Diane almost a decade ago. I'd designed a ring, and every major publication in the area had run the story. *Jewelry Empire Heir Engaged.* The *Diane* is still one of our bestselling engagement rings. Probably partially because of the romantic lore surrounding it.

I grimace at what the headlines will say now.

And besides, as much as I hate Diane right now for what she's done to me, deep down, I don't want her name dragged through the mud like I know it could be. I simply want to part ways and never think of this again. Move on.

We just need to figure out how best to do that without causing attention.

The idea of a rebound reenters my mind, and my attention flicks back to that new sales associate we'd hired today.

Emma Hayes.

Damn, she was cute. Long, wavy hair—a shade of red I don't think I've ever seen. Even under that suffocating blouse she was wearing, I could tell she had nice curves. And that smile?

I shake my head. I'm just horny. And sad. And lonely. Emma works for me. And is fully off limits. And looks to be barely out of college. Jesus.

Although I suppose it doesn't hurt to admire from a distance. Respectfully, that is.

I'm going to have to be careful with that one.

I sigh, standing up and taking my empty can to the recycling basket under my sink, readying myself for yet another lonely night ahead of me.

Chapter 3

Emma

I stare down at the text from Justin on my phone screen. A pit of dread forms in my stomach, and I toss the phone onto my couch.

He's been texting me for the last few days, wanting to talk. And I've been ignoring him.

I know it won't do us any good. We've had more than enough conversations. Conversations with him begging me to take him back, conversations with him berating me for being a bitch and leaving, conversations wanting to dissect our relationship and try again. We've had more than enough conversations for both of us to find closure. Anything more just isn't needed.

In fact, anything more is just painful and scary and frustrating.

But it seems like the longer I ignore him, the more persistent he becomes.

I hear my phone vibrate from the couch, and I heave an irritated sigh while digging through the fridge to try and drum up some ingredients for dinner.

I hear my phone vibrate again. And again. And again. And then I realize he must be calling me. I let it vibrate away, and finally it stops. But then, barely thirty seconds later, it starts up again.

I sigh angrily, stalking across the apartment to grab my phone, glaring down at the screen. Giving in, I answer.

"What, Justin?" I snap.

"God, finally. Why haven't you been responding to my texts?"

"Why do you think?" I retort.

"Look, we need to talk. Can I come over?"

"No."

"Come on, Em. I know what apartment complex you're in, I just need the number."

"How do you know that?" I demand.

"I asked around."

I glare at the wall ahead of me, wondering which of our mutual friends snitched on me. "Justin, we've already gone over everything there is to go over, there's no use in—"

"It's not about getting back together," he interrupts me. "I promise. I know it's over. I just … want some closure."

I pause, unsure whether to believe him. Does he really mean it? "I, uh …"

"Come on, Em. Let me just get a bit of closure. It's the least you owe me," he says.

"Well …"

"What's your apartment number?"

I don't respond.

"I'm already outside the building, Em. Just lemme know the number."

He's here? He's outside? I bite my lip. Damnit. "204," I finally mutter.

"I'll be right there." And with that, he hangs up.

I barely have time to register what I've just agreed to before a loud knock sounds at my door. I shake my head, opening it up to see Justin standing on the threshold. He smiles warily. "It's great to see you, Em."

I wish he'd stop calling me that. Like he still owns me or something.

He steps into the apartment, shutting the door behind him. We stand in awkward silence for a few moments, until finally, he breaks it.

"I heard you got a new job."

My heart sinks at that. I eye him warily. "Yeah …"

"Bishop Jewelers," he says.

Okay, so he knows. I bite my lip, preparing myself for anything. That's the thing with Justin. He could be totally fine about something, or he could end up flipping out. You never knew.

"You know, considering how you just up and left me, there is one big thing you could do to help with *closure*," he says.

I narrow my eyes at him. Both at the implication that my leaving was heartless, and at the suspicion as to what he's going to suggest. "What do you want, Justin?" I ask quietly.

"I want to fuck up Bishop Jewelers, and you're the way to do it," he states simply.

I stare at him for a few heartbeats. "What?" is what I finally come up with.

"You heard me."

I shake my head, feeling the exasperation coming on. "What are you talking about?"

"You know they're the reason Stoll Jewelry went out of business. It's bad enough that you jumped ship and went straight to them—but now you can actually do some good—"

"Stoll went under for a lot of reasons, Justin, you know that," I interrupt.

"Bishop Jewelers being the main one!" he snaps. "They're a fucking conglomerate. They squash the little guys. Well, it's time for the little guys to get revenge."

"Revenge?" I echo, trying to piece together whatever crazy plan Justin has come up with.

He nods. "Yes. At first, I was furious to learn that you'd taken a job with them, but now? Now, it's the perfect in."

I'm already shaking my head. "I'm not spying on them for you or anything like that."

"Good, because that's not what I want."

"Well, then what—"

"I want you to seduce the owner."

A long pause stretches between us, his words echoing in the stillness around us. Finally, a laugh bubbles up from deep within me. "Are you serious?"

It's quite possibly the most absurd thing I've ever heard come out of Justin's mouth. And he's said quite a few absurd things.

But he doesn't laugh along. He simply stares me down, unmoving. "Yes, I'm serious. Ezra Bishop. The owner, CEO, or whatever. He's married, and he's the perfect face to their perfect company—one of their engagement rings is even named after his wife."

I balk a bit at the news that Ezra is married. I don't remember seeing a ring on his finger the other day when I'd met him. But that doesn't matter. "This is insane," I say through another laugh.

"I want to see their pristine reputation ruined. I want the headlines to be littered with stories about how Ezra, the perfect face of Bishop Jewelers, cheated on his wife with a lowly sales associate."

"Justin, people cheat all the time," I say, rolling my eyes. "This isn't going to ruin their business, and more importantly—it isn't going to bring Stoll's back."

"I don't care that it won't ruin it—I still want it tarnished," Justin presses.

I shake my head, growing tired of this conversation. "You know I'm not going to *seduce* anyone."

"Oh yes, you are," Justin says, his gaze darkening. "And *this* is why." He pulls out his phone, pressing something and then holding it out for me to see.

23

It's the sound that registers first. Moaning.

I'm confused at first, but then, all at once, it hits me. It's *my* voice. Moaning, whimpering, saying Justin's name.

My eyes widen, and I lurch forward to catch a glimpse of mine and Justin's naked bodies before he snatches the phone away from me.

"When did you take that?" My blood runs cold. I don't ever remember us filming ourselves. At least, we'd never discussed filming ourselves. Had he done this … without telling me?

Obviously.

He smirks, turning off the video and sliding it into his pocket. "You turn Ezra Bishop into a dirty cheater, or I post this video on every social media platform in existence," he says simply.

I feel like my body has been submerged in ice. I stare at Justin in disbelief. He can't be serious. He can't. Sure, Justin was an asshole, but he'd never do this. He wouldn't.

"Justin," I say slowly. "Please …"

He cocks his head. "The choice is yours, Em."

Em. The word makes my blood boil coming from his mouth. "What if I can't do it?" I ask. "It's very likely he won't fall for it."

Justin shoots me a look. "Come on. A hot piece of meat like you? Any guy would trip over himself drooling just to get a good look at you. Flash him your tits, and you're in."

My face flushes red at the implications. "You know this won't really hurt them. They're an empire. It'll only end up with me losing my job and Ezra losing his marriage," I say, my voice choking.

"Well, I'd like to see you lose your job and Ezra lose his marriage, then," he replies coldly.

I glare at him, running in circles in my mind trying to find a way out—and ending up stuck. There *is* no way out. If I don't want that humiliating video out there for everyone to see; I have to do what Justin asks.

"I'll call you next week to check in on your progress," Justin says, turning toward the door.

I want to call out to him, to plead him to change his mind, to not make me do this, but I find that I've lost my voice. And besides, deep down, I know it's no use.

The door slams behind him, and I'm left in the silence of my apartment. It isn't until the shock and panic subside that I finally crumple to the floor in sobs.

Chapter 4

Ezra

I sit in my office at Bishop Jewelers, staring off, lost in thought. Through the doorway, I can see all the way to the front room where Rachel and Emma are speaking with a few customers. The store seems as busy as ever.

I glance back to my computer, to the new design mockups I'd been sent. They're beautiful, but I'm just not feeling the pull I'd been hoping for. But I don't know, maybe I've lost my touch. Maybe I'm looking for the wrong things. Part of me simply wants to find a new design to finally outsell the *Diane*, to get that stupid ring away from me—to never have to look at it again. I'd love a reason to pull it completely, but with it being one of our bestsellers, I can't justify it.

So if I could just come up with a better, more brilliant, more successful design, that could be my ticket. Get Diane, her ring, and her memory out of my life for good.

I scroll through the designs again. They're all nice. Trendy. Elegant. Lots of emerald cuts and beautifully-shaped bands. We could do with a few more trendy items.

A noise from the doorway pulls my attention upward. I raise an eyebrow in surprise. "Emma," I greet.

She smiles at me, pushing a lock of her long, ginger hair behind her ear. "Are you busy?" she asks.

I sigh, leaning back in my chair. "Not overly, no."

She comes closer. She rounds the desk, catching a glimpse of the designs on my computer and looking closer. "Oh wow," she breathes. "Those are beautiful."

She leans forward, and I'm suddenly very aware of the low-cut top she's wearing, how it gaps, the perfect round tops of her breasts on full display. I find my breath quickening, my eyes glued to her cleavage. Damn what I wouldn't do to see more of her.

I clear my throat, horrified at my inappropriate thoughts, pulling my gaze away from her. "Yeah, they're uh …" I stammer. "Jason, our designer—have you met him yet? He came up with these."

She shakes her head without straightening up, the movement making her breasts jiggle slightly.

Fuck.

"Do you ever design anything?" she asks. She finally straightens up—thank god or I might end up humiliating myself by actually drooling over her. But to my further surprise, she spins around and takes a casual seat on my desk, planting herself barely a foot away from me. The movement has her skirt sliding up, revealing her knee and the bottom of her thigh.

And as if a moth drawn to a flame, my gaze is pinned there.

Jesus, am I this horny and starved for attention that I can't keep my eyes off my new sales associate? She is about one of the prettiest women I've ever encountered though. That gorgeous red hair, that cute smile, that figure that has me imagining dirty, dirty things.

"I don't design as much anymore, but yes," I answer, my voice feeling husky.

"Ooh, I'd love to see your designs," she says.

At first, I want to suggest going out to the floor where she can see an array of rings I'd designed a few years back, but to my absolute horror, I can feel the proof of my arousal in my pants. There's no way in hell I can stand up now. Instead, I reach for a nearby Bishop Jewelers catalog on my desk, thumbing through the pages until I find one with a display of engagement rings I'd designed somewhat recently. I flip the catalog around so she can see. "These are mine," I state simply.

Her eyes widen as she gingerly takes the catalog from me. "Wow," she breathes. "These are … gorgeous."

I can feel myself flushing ever so slightly. Jesus Christ. What's wrong with me? Since when did I blush at compliments? Since when did the presence of a pretty, young woman get me so riled up? Is it her? Or am I just sad and lonely as fuck?

"You're really talented," she says genuinely, handing the catalog back to me. "I can see how the company has done so well."

"Thank you," I say, both shocked at and trying to hide how much her compliment means to me.

"Emma!" Rachel calls from the floor. "Can you come help me with some inventory?"

Emma stands quickly. "Yes, coming!" she calls, striding toward the door. She shoots me a soft smile over her shoulder that does alarmingly reactive things to my body.

God, what is it with this girl? What is it about her that I find so alluring?

29

I shake my head, trying to get the images of her breasts and legs out of my head so I can focus back on work.

Chapter 5

Emma

It's Friday night, and like every night this week, I
get home to my apartment, toss my purse on the couch,
and immediately curl up in bed. My stomach is in a
constant state of knots. I've barely eaten all week. A
mixture of emotions wash through me—rage,
humiliation, denial, despair.

Because I truly can't think of any way out of this.
I have to do what Justin wants. I have to.

There's no way I could live through those videos
being leaked online. The humiliation would kill me.

So here I am, shamelessly *flirting* with my boss at
every opportunity. Humiliation burns through me at the

thought of it. Of how I'd handled myself this week. Practically throwing myself at Ezra.

The buzzing of my phone catches my attention, and I grab it to see that Justin is calling me. The pit in my stomach grows. I want nothing more than to throw my phone at the wall, but I'm worried about what he might do if I don't answer.

So I do.

"What?"

"How's it going?" he asks simply.

"I'm working on it," I reply.

"Any progress?"

"It's going to take time, okay? Back off."

There's a long pause. "Just don't let it take too long," Justin finally responds.

"I'm trying as hard as I can, okay? You just need to be patient."

He sighs through the phone. "Fine." With that, he hangs up.

I throw my phone angrily to the end of my bed, feeling another rush of tears coming on. You'd think I'd have cried out all the water in my body this week.

Continued doubts seep into my brain about whether or not I can actually pull this off. I think back to the handful of interactions I'd had with Ezra this week. Sure, he seems attracted to me—that's not hard to gauge. But to cheat on his wife? Would he really consider that? The idea of being a homewrecker makes me feel sick. But the idea of those videos of me being out there for the whole world to see makes me sicker.

■ ı

After Justin sends me a screenshot of the video he plans to leak—every feature of my face and body humiliatingly on display, I'm spurred into action, and I come into the shop Monday morning with a plan.

My stomach is in knots. So much so that I purposefully didn't bring a lunch, knowing there's no way I'll be able to keep it down. Both from the dread and self-loathing and from the actual plan I'm trying to enact.

"You okay?" Rachel asks me a few hours into the day.

I force a smile onto my face. "Yeah, just didn't sleep well last night. A little out of it," I lie, making a mental note to try and conceal my nerves better.

But when Ezra comes into the shop in the early afternoon, it only makes my anxieties worse. I shoot him what I hope is a flirtatious smile over the counter, and he grins back, sweeping past me and into the back room where his office is.

My plan can't start until the end of the day, so I spend the rest of the afternoon keeping my head down and working.

When six o'clock rolls around, I turn to Rachel. "I can finish up the bookkeeping if you want to head out," I offer.

Her face lights up. "You sure?"

I nod. "Yeah, I've seen you do it enough times that I can probably handle it. Besides, Ezra's in the back if I need help."

"Great, thanks," she says, grabbing her purse from the back room. "See you tomorrow." She waves and is out the door.

I glance over my shoulder. When Ezra comes into the shop, he usually arrives in the early afternoon and stays—well, I'm not exactly sure how late he stays. All I know is that he's always still here when the sales associates leave.

I turn off the sign and lock the door, heading to the computer behind the reception area to fill out the day's logs—recording sales and making sure all the cash is arranged as it should be. It only takes me a few minutes, but I stick around later, my nerves rising by the second.

I glance at the clock. 6:30. I close my eyes, taking a deep breath. Every bone in my body is screaming no, that I should absolutely not go through with my plan. But I can't help but think about that screenshot Justin sent me, the echoes of my moans when he'd played the video in my apartment. I imagine it all over Facebook, Instagram—my friends and family seeing it. I imagine it on revenge porn sites—plastered there until the ends of eternity.

Fuck.

I have to do this.

I force my legs to do my bidding, moving into the back room and softly knocking on the door to Ezra's office.

"Come in," his deep voice calls.

I turn the knob, stepping into the room. "Hi," I say quietly.

"Emma." He raises an eyebrow. "I'd assumed you and Rachel would be gone by now."

"Yeah …" I bite my lip. "Um, actually … my car's having issues. And the Uber rates are insane this time of day." I make an apologetic face. "Is there any way you'd be able to give me a ride home?"

Surprise flashes across his face, then understanding. "Oh. Yes, of course." He glances back at his computer momentarily. "I was just about done here anyway. Let me just finish up this email."

I stand awkwardly in the doorway while he types away. I try to internally calm my nerves, reminding myself that I'm supposed to be sexy right now, that I need to appear calm, confident, alluring.

Ezra snaps his laptop shut and stands, shooting me a smile. "Are you ready to go?" he asks, putting his laptop into his briefcase.

I nod, clutching my purse to my side.

"Great." He grabs his keys from the desk and then moves to leave the room. I'm still standing in the doorway, and I force myself not to move, meaning he has to brush past me in order to get out. His arm grazes my shoulder, and I smell the scent of his cologne. Something like sandalwood.

I follow him out into the shop where he walks over to the wall and flicks off a few lights, leaving us in slight darkness.

His gaze catches mine for a moment, and it's almost as if time stands still, my breath frozen in my throat—nothing matters except for the glint in his eyes, the tension in the air around us.

But he quickly breaks that spell and stalks across the room toward the front door. I hurry after him. We step out into the cool autumn evening. The sun is just about to set as we walk down Newbury Street.

"I love the sunsets here," I say quietly, walking beside him.

He nods, smiling softly. "Yeah. Something about the way the city glows … it's always mesmerized me."

"I'm assuming you grew up here?" I ask.

"Yeah. Beacon Hill area. I grew up coming into the shop and watching my grandfather work on jewelry designs." He chuckles softly. "So this sunset walk is a very familiar one."

I look ahead, watching the orange glow as it spreads across the city.

"Are you from here too?" he asks.

"Basically. Grew up in Waltham and moved to the city for school. Then I just stayed." I leave out the part about the abusive ex-boyfriend and how my last job closed down. How I'd hoped this would be a fresh new start for me when it's actually turning into a complete nightmare. I swallow the lump forming in my throat.

"How do you like it?" Ezra asks. "The city, I mean."

I don't know how to answer. Mainly because so much of Boston has been associated with Justin, with Stoll Jewelers. And now this. Maybe I should have stayed in my tiny hometown. "I love it," I lie, turning to him with a smile. "I absolutely love it."

He smiles back at me, and it's then that I notice a dimple on the right side of his face. Just the right side. So adorably uneven.

We reach his car and, to my surprise, he opens my door for me, gesturing me in. I raise an eyebrow at him. "What a gentleman," I tease.

He laughs. "What can I say? My mother taught me right." He closes the door and comes around, climbing into the driver's seat.

Suddenly inside a car with the man, I can't help but realize how close of quarters we're in. We're barely a foot away from each other. Close enough to … do the things Justin wants from me.

"Want to plug your address into Google Maps?" Ezra asks, handing over his phone.

My fingers brush lightly against his as I take his phone, sending shivers up my spine. I quickly type in my address and hand the phone back.

We drive down the streets of Boston in silence for a few moments, and I start out the window at the passing buildings. I feel like my body is on fire. Like the world is about to implode. Is the tension just on my side, or can he feel it too?

I glance sideways at him. He has both hands on the steering wheel, and he's looking straight ahead. He seems calm. I stare at the outline of his jaw, how it seems chiseled out of stone. At the gray smattering of hair at his temples.

"So what do you do besides run the most successful jewelry empire on the east coast?" I ask, placing my elbow on the center console and leaning toward him.

A quiet chuckle escapes him. "Not much, really," he answers, keeping his eyes on the road.

"Oh, come on, there must be something," I press.

He stares ahead in thought for a moment. "I enjoy reading," he finally says.

"Reading?" I echo. I'm actually kind of surprised. I never pegged him for the book type. And I never would have guessed that we share a core interest. Especially one as mundane as reading. "What kind of books do you read?"

He glances sideways at me, and the look makes my heart jump in my chest. He's smiling, smirking, like he doesn't want to answer. "Dumb things," he says.

I laugh out loud. "Okay, now you have to tell me more."

His grin widens, and he shakes his head. "Your average airport read." He shrugs. "A thriller, a mystery, fantasy. I've …" He chuckles again. "I've even been known to read a romance from time to time."

I raise my eyebrows. "A romance reader?" I laugh. "Ezra Bishop, quite possibly the richest man in Boston, spends his time reading trashy romance novels?"

"Hey, I said nothing about trashy," he responds with a laugh.

"To be fair, I'm also a romance reader—I just never thought I'd meet a man with the same hobby."

He smirks. "I love a good story. I can't help it if sometimes that comes in the form of romance."

It's just now that I realize we're coming up on my apartment building. Ezra turns into the parking lot, pulling up in front of the front door and putting the car in park.

My nerves bundle in my lower stomach. I'd been so engrossed in our conversation that I'd almost forgotten what I'd set out to do. I glance at my apartment building in trepidation.

I turn to Ezra, offering a shy smile. "Thanks for the ride," I say quietly.

He smiles in return. "Any time."

"I, uh …" I hesitate, glancing up to meet his eyes. What I see there is sincerity, possibly even genuine attraction. I can tell he likes me—at least as a person. And I know he's attracted to me. But will he be receptive to what I have to say next? "Do you want to come up?" I force the question out before I have time to second guess myself.

Surprise flashes across his features, and I immediately feel my stomach drop. Time seems to slow, every second passing as if it were an eternity. He opens his mouth, closes his mouth, opens it again.

"I'm married." The words echo in the space around us, and humiliation burns through me.

"Oh, I …" I stutter, my mind running a million miles an hour. Every part of me wants to shut this down, to apologize, to run upstairs to my apartment and forget this ever happened. Because of course he's married. I *know* he's married. And what I'm doing is quite possibly the worst thing anyone could do.

And it doesn't matter that Justin is about to ruin my life with those videos. It doesn't mean I can just go around and ruin other people's.

This was a horrible, horrible mistake.

"I'm so sorry," I say, shaking my head, reaching for the door handle.

"No." Ezra reaches out to put a hand on my arm, stopping me. His touch sends shivers across my skin. "I know you didn't know—I haven't been wearing my ring. I …" He sighs, and I force myself to turn and meet his gaze. "My wife and I are separated. You didn't do anything wrong."

His words come crashing down on me. Separated. In all honesty, I hadn't even noticed he wasn't wearing a ring. I knew he was married because Justin told me so, and I'd been so caught up in everything else, that I'd never even thought to glance at his ring finger.

A silence stretches between us, so long I think it might just go on forever. Finally, Ezra breaks it. "I'll come in," he says quietly, his dark eyes meeting mine. "Just for one drink."

Chapter 6

Emma

My hands are practically shaking as I unlock the door to my apartment and step through, Ezra following. My brain keeps repeating the last few minutes over and over again in my mind. From humiliation to relief to … attraction?

The fact that Ezra and his wife are separated completely changes everything. For one, it removes the guilt of being a potential homewrecker. And suddenly I'm looking at him in a whole new light. Obviously, I noticed how attractive he was before, but now I'm *noticing*.

I gesture nervously to the couch while I head to the kitchen to pull out two wine glasses from the cabinet. "Red wine okay?" I call.

"Sounds great," Ezra replies.

I hurriedly pour two glasses and take a seat next to him on the couch. We sit awkwardly for a moment, before Ezra breaks the silence with, "So, is this how the romance books you read all start?"

I feel myself blushing, and I bite my lip. "Maybe," I answer.

He smirks down at his wine glass. "I'm surprised," he finally says.

I furrow my brows. "By what?"

He looks up to meet my gaze, cocking his head just a bit. "Your attraction," he says bluntly. He doesn't say it in a self-deprecating way. Not like he has any lack of confidence. He simply stares at me as if trying to solve a puzzle.

Electricity shoots through me by the way he's looking at me. "Who wouldn't be attracted to you?" I say, but my voice comes out almost as a whisper, and I can feel my blush growing deeper.

He doesn't answer, simply takes a sip of his wine. Afterward, he shakes his head slowly. "Emma, I don't know if we should—"

Panic sets in, and I stand suddenly. "I'll be right back," I tell Ezra, halting what he was going to say.

I leave the living room, entering my bathroom and locking the door behind me. I stand in front of the mirror, staring myself down for a good ten seconds, and then I take a deep breath.

I think about the next part of this plan. The final part. The part I'd been most nervous about, but an aspect I assumed would be impossible for most men to turn down. The idea of it sets my heart beating out of my chest, but after what Ezra was just about to say out there, I think I need to lay all my cards on the table.

You can do this, Emma, I tell myself. *It's now or never.*

I swallow, close my eyes, and nod to myself. Then I start stripping. I pull my dress over my head, then busy myself with removing my bra and panties until I'm standing in front of the mirror wearing absolutely nothing.

I bite my lip, the nerves in my stomach multiplying by the second. I reach into my drawer, pulling out some lip gloss and blush and reapplying. I run my fingers through my hair, enhancing the curls. I look over myself. While I've always been a bit self-conscious about my body, I do know that I'm conventionally attractive. My breasts are large and full, and I have an hourglass figure.

I can feel the panic rising within me, so before I can change my mind, I grab the door handle and step out into the living room.

Ezra looks up when he hears me enter the room, and his jaw immediately goes slack. He stares at me for a long moment, his gaze sliding along my body, lingering on my breasts that are currently rising and falling with my breath.

He stands slowly, placing the wine glass on the coffee table. He meets my gaze, his eyes filled with confusion, but also curiosity and the telltale signs of attraction. "Emma ..." he says slowly.

The way he says my name has my nipples hardening, and I take in a shaky breath.

"What are you doing?" he asks, a slight smirk playing across his face.

I step toward him, spanning the distance between us until I'm barely a foot away from him, looking up into his eyes. "You know what I'm doing," I breathe, reaching up to run my fingers through his hair.

He leans into my hand, his mouth opening just barely. His gaze slides lazily across my body again, taking me in.

I run my hand down the side of his face, his neck, to his chest.

Suddenly, he reaches out to grasp my wrist, and I freeze. This is it. It's happening. I swallow, forcing myself to remain calm.

"Emma," he says again, and I'm beginning to love the sound of my name coming from his lips. "Do you really want to do this?" There's a seriousness in his gaze.

I nod, even though my reasons are far more complicated than he could ever know. "Yes," I say, reaching for him with my other hand.

But he takes that one too, and suddenly he has both my wrists locked under his control, and he's boring a hole into my soul with his gaze. A small smile creeps across his face. He leans toward me, close enough that the tips of my nipples brush against his chest, sending a wave of arousal through me. His lips brush against my ear, and he whispers, "I know you're trying to take control." His grip on my wrists tightens ever so slightly. "But *I* like being the one in control."

He leans back, his eyes on mine again. Gone is the polite, gentlemanly Ezra Bishop, and in his place is a man who looks ready to devour me with just his gaze. My core tightens, and I feel my pussy getting wet.

Fuck. What does that mean? Whatever it means, I'm ready to find out.

But Ezra does the last thing I expect. He lets go of me. He steps back.

I stand there, shocked while he shoots me a smirk. "I take the reins, or we don't do this."

I find myself with no other option than to nod, suddenly overcome with the humiliating fact that I'm standing here naked before him and we aren't … *doing anything*. And the longer we go without doing anything, the more humiliating it becomes. *Touch me*, my body begs him. *Touch me now*. Everywhere. All at once.

"Good girl."

My mouth drops open, and a fire alights in my lower belly.

"We'll fuck when I say we're going to fuck," he says simply. He spans the distance between us, brushing his lips gently across mine. But just as quickly as they're there, his lips are gone, and he's turning toward the couch, grabbing his coat, and heading for the door.

I watch him go in complete shock. The door shuts behind him, leaving me alone and naked in my apartment.

Chapter 7

Ezra

I can think of nothing other than Emma Hayes all night long. Her eyes, her hair, her legs, her breasts. Every inch of her. How I'd so badly wanted to take her right then and there, savor every second of it, make her mine.

I'm still in utter disbelief that the evening played out the way it did. I'd gone from halfheartedly fantasizing about my attractive new sales assistant to having her suddenly standing before me, utterly naked and willing to do whatever I wanted.

And I'd walked out the door.

The absurdity of it almost makes me laugh. A beautiful woman had basically thrown herself at me, and I'd walked away.

But I have my reasons, and I'm standing by them. Because what I'd told her was true. I may give off the kind, unassuming gentleman demeanor, but in bed, I like to do things a certain way. And that certain way means I'm in charge.

Of everything.

Of when she's naked, of what we do, how I touch her, of when she comes. Everything.

And I'd love nothing more than to be in charge of Emma. Telling her what to do and having her obey at a moment's notice. And in order to get what I wanted, I needed to turn the tables. Get the upper hand and take things from there.

And after seeing that look on her face—shock, embarrassment, confusion—I know that everything I want will eventually fall into place.

I lean back against the pillows on my bed, staring out the window to the city lights outside. I'd been toying with the idea of a rebound. Something to get my mind off Diane, help me move on, help me heal. And maybe this just might be it.

The next morning, I push open the door to Bishop Jewelers, the soft bell echoing throughout the shop. Rachel looks up when she sees me, confusion clouding her features. "You're not usually in on Tuesdays," she says simply.

I shrug. "Decided I wanted to work from the shop today," I say. "Where's Emma?"

Rachel inclines her head to the back room. I stride past the counter and through the door. Emma is busy making herself a coffee in the kitchenette in the corner, her back to me. I take the moment to check her out— how her pencil skirt seems to hug her curves so perfectly. My mind jumps back to last night—to what it was like to see those curves unclothed.

"Do you know if we have any creamer?" Emma asks, turning. But when her eyes land on me, she straightens, immediately putting her coffee down. "I thought you were Rachel," she says quickly.

"Can I speak to you in my office?" I ask.

She nods, suddenly looking terrified, and I feel a tiny twinge of guilt. I really shouldn't be trying to scare her.

She follows me into my office, and I shut the door behind her. She stands quietly, watching me warily.

"You're not in trouble, Emma," I say, unable to take that look on her face any longer. In fact, this is partly why I decided to come in today and have this conversation.

I can see the relief washing over her features, and I wonder if she spent all night worrying. Now I feel bad about how I'd walked out.

I approach her, moving to stand just inches away from her. "I very much want to continue whatever this is," I say softly, reaching up to brush a strand of hair behind her ear. "But I want to make it very clear that regardless of what happens—what we do or don't do—your job will never be in jeopardy. I need to establish this before we move forward."

She widens her eyes slightly in surprise, and then she shoots me a small smile. "Understood, Mr. Bishop."

I clench my jaw. Damn. *Mr. Bishop.* "I normally like being called Ezra, but I like Mr. Bishop when it's coming from your mouth," I say, leaning down to press a soft kiss to the nape of her neck.

She sighs quietly, and fuck does that sound do something to me. I have half a mind to take her right here and now.

"I mean what I said," I say, trailing kisses up her neck and breathing against her ear, "about being in control."

52

Her breathing becomes ragged, and I feel her gripping the front of my shirt.

"Will you do what you're told?" I whisper.

"Yes," she breathes, almost immediately.

I smile. Fuck, she's obedient, and I fucking love it. I lean back far enough to meet her gaze. "I don't want you to come until I make you come. Understand?"

Her eyes widen, and her mouth opens.

I raise my eyebrows. "Understand?" I repeat.

She nods.

"It means no going home and thinking about everything I'm going to do to you while you get yourself off. And it definitely means no letting any other man lay his hands on you."

She nods again, her chest rising and falling. Damn, she's turned on by this. She's not just agreeing to my terms, she's enjoying them. "Is that a yes?" I prompt.

"Yes," she says.

I smile. "Good girl."

Her eyes darken, and it takes every ounce of self-control within me to take step back. "Let me buy you a drink this weekend. Friday?"

"Okay," she breathes.

"I'll look forward to it," I say, leaning in to press a kiss to her cheek before opening my office door and gesturing her back out to the floor. "Don't forget your promise," I tell her.

She steps out on wobbly legs, glancing back at me over her shoulder.

"Oh, and the creamer is on the bottom shelf in the fridge."

Chapter 8

Emma

I find myself at the end of the day sitting on my couch, staring ahead blankly, the shock of the last twenty-four hours refusing to subside.

When Ezra had called me into his office, I was sure I was about to be fired. After that humiliating display last night—basically throwing myself at him and having him walk out? Not to mention the fact that he's technically my boss and this is a million different types of inappropriate.

But instead, he'd shocked me even further. By doing just about the hottest thing I could imagine.

And then forbidding me from …

I blush just thinking about it. Holy shit. Shit, shit, shit. I can't stop thinking about him. About how fucking sexy he was in his office laying down the rules and telling me to obey. About how much I want him to follow through with that promise, about how I can hardly wait to see him again.

My mind wanders back to the way his lips had felt brushing against the sensitive skin of my neck, how deep his voice had sounded in my ear, the way I imagine his fingers would feel on my bare skin.

I can feel a moistness blooming between my legs, and I bite my lip, practically whining in frustration.

Ezra's rule. His one, stupid rule. And despite the fact that I could lie, somehow I know that he'd see right through it.

I shake my head and force myself to stand, heading to the kitchen for a glass of water.

I muddle through the rest of the week in a sort of daze. Every time the door to the shop rings, I look up, hoping to see Ezra, even though I know full well he typically only comes in on Mondays. I'm acting like such a ditz that even Rachel notices, asking if everything's alright with me. I brush it off, telling her I haven't slept well, hoping she'll buy the lie.

But as the days wear on, I find it harder and harder to concentrate. Both from the fact that I'm finding myself increasingly attracted to Ezra, and because of his final rule. The rule that makes him all the more infuriatingly hot.

On Friday, he sends me a text from his private phone with an address.

Ezra: I'll send a car for you at 8 p.m.

Oh yeah. He probably thinks my car is still "not working." I'm utterly unable to focus the rest of the day. All I can think about is how badly I want him to fulfill his promise. God, I'm so turned on by the thought of him that maybe even just his touch could send me over the edge.

"You've been so off this week," Rachel says with a laugh when I accidentally drop our new shipment of shopping bags all over the floor.

I laugh nervously. "Yeah, just some personal stuff going on," I say, hoping she'll drop it.

Her brows furrow. "Nothing bad, I hope."

I shrug. "Nothing terrible, I just … need to get it sorted out."

She nods. "Well, I hope the weekend off will help."

At five o'clock sharp, I'm out the door, heading back to my apartment as quickly as possible. I shower and blow-dry my hair, then spend what feels like an eternity going through absolutely every outfit I own and deciding that all of them are terrible. I want to look sexy, but not too sexy. I want to fit the vibe but not look like I'm trying to hard.

I finally settle on a classic black dress. It falls to about mid-thigh, and it has a v-neck deep enough to be sexy but not so much that it's slutty. Although I don't know, maybe slutty is what I should be going for.

By the time I finish doing my hair and makeup, I get a notification that my Uber has arrived.

I grab my purse and slide on some black kitten heels and head out the door.

On the drive over, my stomach is doing summersaults. I'm so dizzy with excitement, anxiety, and lust that I feel my head might explode. When the car pulls up in front of a gorgeous old brownstone in Beacon Hill, I raise an eyebrow in surprise. Is this Ezra's home?

Although now that I think about it, of course we couldn't go out to an actual restaurant or bar. He's still technically married to his wife.

That reminder sends a shockwave through me, and suddenly it all comes back. The reason I'm doing this in the first place. It's crazy, but I'd almost forgotten the deal I'd made with Justin. I'd been so caught up in Ezra, that my attraction to him had taken center stage.

The driver clears his throat, pulling me from my thoughts. I thank him quickly and get out of the car, walking up to the enormous brownstone and pressing the button outside the door.

Ezra's voice immediately comes through the speakers. "Come in and take the elevator to the top floor," he says.

The door buzzes, and I reach for the handle to find it unlocked. I step inside to find a gorgeously decorated entryway with a small elevator to the right. I follow Ezra's instructions and step inside, pressing the button for the top floor. My nerves tangle in my stomach as the elevator ascends, and then with a ding, it comes to a stop and the doors slide open.

I step out into an open space with a kitchen on one side and couches and lounge chairs on the other. The exposed brick on the walls is a beautiful deep red, with huge bay windows looking out into the street below, with city lights beyond.

My gaze lands on Ezra, who stands when he sees me enter. He shoots me a warm smile and approaches, holding out a glass of red wine.

"I know I promised to buy you a drink," he says, handing me the glass and leaning in to press a soft kiss to my cheek. "But I figured we'd be more comfortable here."

Somehow his presence seems to put a lot of my nerves to rest, even though the anticipation remains.

He inclines his head toward the other side of the room and leads me over to a couch near the window. I sit first, and then he does, his leg brushing against mine.

"How do you like the wine?" he asks after I've taken my first sip.

I nod. "It's good." I can tell it's much more expensive than the types of wine I drink. There's just something about it. "I normally just drink bottom shelf red blends," I say with a laugh.

He chuckles, taking a sip of his own.

I glance around the room, unable to not notice how well it's decorated. I think back to his wife. Or ex-wife? What did he say? That they were separated? I wonder if she decorated this place. Or, I suppose, he could have hired an interior designer.

"You like the art?" Ezra asks after a moment of silence, a smirk on his face.

I laugh, feeling embarrassed for my obvious perusal. "Yes, it's … homey. But in an upscale way."

He snorts. "Well, thank you."

"I …" I begin but then think better of it. But Ezra already has an eyebrow raised, prompting me to continue. I sigh. "Your wife," I reluctantly say.

His smirk leaves, replaced by an understanding grimace. He nods. "Yes. I should probably explain that."

"You don't have to if you're not comfortable," I say quickly, but he's already shaking his head.

"No, you deserve to know," he insists. He takes a moment to compose himself, taking a sip of wine before placing his glass on the coffee table in front of us. "Diane and I are separated," he says simply. "So separated, in fact, that she's currently living with another man."

My eyes widen in surprise. Holy shit. His wife … left him? For someone else?

"Oh my god," I say quietly. "I'm so sorry."

He smiles softly. "It's okay. She says she's happier. And I'm … well, I'm managing."

A long pause stretches between us. Suddenly I wonder whether all of this changes Justin's plans. If Ezra isn't with his wife anymore, then being seen with me isn't much of a scandal at all.

"We haven't officially announced any kind of separation yet, and I still have yet to file the papers," he continues. He shakes his head. "I know how the public perceives me—and Diane and our relationship. News of her cheating on me? She'd be destroyed in the media. And as hurt as I am … I don't want to do that to her."

My hope from seconds ago slowly vanishes. While Ezra might technically be separated, he's also still technically married. And doesn't seem to be ready to change that any time soon.

I nod along. "That makes sense. But I'm sorry that you really get the short end of the stick here."

He pauses, seemingly lost in thought. Then his gaze raises to mine, pinning me to my seat. "I wouldn't say it's all bad," he finally says.

I can feel my cheeks heating up, and I look away, taking a sip of wine.

"How about you? Any sordid love affairs ending up flames?" he asks with a chuckle.

I shrug. "No cheating scandals. Just an ex-boyfriend who …" I trail off, knowing I can't tell him the actual truth of my struggles. That Justin is more than just an awful ex. That he's turned into a blackmailer. Someone threatening to leak intimate videos of me, create fucking revenge porn out of our private moments. Someone who's actions are forcing me to fuck over people who don't deserve it.

I feel something wet slide down my cheek, and to my utter horror, I realize I'm crying. I lift a hand to my cheek in shock, wiping the tear away quickly.

"Oh shit, Emma," Ezra says quickly, reaching for me. "I was joking. I hoped my situation was unique." He gives a humorless chuckle.

I shake my head, trying to brush it off. "No, no, I'm fine. I just ... my recent ex wasn't very nice to me, that's all."

Suddenly Ezra's arms are wrapping around me, pulling me against his chest. His embrace suddenly makes me want to cry harder, but I resist the urge, holding the tears back as best I can.

"Well, he's an absolute shithead," Ezra says, his face muffled against my hair.

I sniffle, nodding against his chest.

We sit like that for a while, Ezra holding me close, rubbing his hand along my back. When we finally pull away, he stares down at me with a furrowed brow, a cross between sadness and concern. "Whatever you went through with him, I'm sorry," he says.

I shake my head, forcing on a smile. "It's okay," I lie. "It's over now."

He smiles, changing the topic to something lighter, asking how my day was at work and what I would normally spend my weekends doing.

By the time we've finished our wine, I'm curled up next to him, giggling over something he just said, surrounded by a warm, fuzzy feeling I think is half part alcohol, half part him.

He twirls a lock of hair around his finger, leaning down to press a soft kiss to the top of my head. "Emma," he says quietly.

I crane my neck to look up at him. "Have you been a good girl?" he asks, and my belly clenches. "Did you do what I asked?"

I nod slowly.

He raises an eyebrow, almost as if he doesn't believe me.

I straighten up. "I did," I insist. "I mean—didn't." I bite my lip. "You know what I mean."

A small smile tugs at the corner of his lips, and he leans toward me. "Who knew you were so perfectly obedient?"

He reaches out to run his thumb over my bottom lip, gently pulling so that my mouth is just barely open. My breath hitches in my throat, my blood roaring in my ears. I'm lost in those eyes of his, pinning me to the spot. I hate to admit it, but he could ask anything of me, and I'd do it. I'm at his complete and utter mercy.

And fuck, does he know it.

He rails his thumb down my face, down the side of my neck, then follows the deep v of my dress, ending right between my breasts, his eyes on mine the whole time.

He reaches for the strap of my dress, gently pulling it over my shoulder. He does the same with the other, and then he takes the top of my dress and begins pulling down.

A nervous flutter overtakes me before I remember that he's already seen me naked before. He's already seen all of me.

He slides the top of my dress down, revealing my full, bare breasts—the nature of the dress didn't allow for a bra.

He takes them in, slowly caressing them one at a time, squeezing and then pinching my nipples. I gasp at the sensation, and his smirk widens. "Fuck, you're beautiful," he says, rubbing circles with his thumbs over my nipples. I moan quietly, throwing my head back.

I can feel the dampness growing between my thighs. I'm so worked up and so deprived, I truly could come just from this. If he just keeps going …

"How do you feel about being a good girl for me one more time?" he asks.

I nod, ready to do anything he asks of me.

He smiles with satisfaction. "And you're okay with me being a bit … dominant?" he asks. "You like that?" He's keeping up that same air of power, but beneath the façade is a genuine question. He wants to make sure I'm okay with this. And despite not truly knowing what all *this* entails, I find myself nodding. Whatever it is, I want more of it. Now.

At my nod, he stands, pulling me with me, and then he places his hands on my shoulders, guiding me to my knees in front of him. I stare up at him, my bare breasts heaving in anticipation as he slowly unbuckles his belt and unzips his pants. He pulls out his cock, and my eyes widen.

Holy shit. Sure, I've given head before, but will that even fit in my mouth?

He strokes it a few times and, taking in my expression, simply says, "You can take it." He reaches down to take a handful of my hair, angling my head upward to meet his gaze. "Tap my leg if you want to stop," he tells me, and then he guides his cock into my mouth.

I take it as deep as I can—which, truthfully, isn't very deep. Keeping his eyes on mine, he slowly slides his cock in and out of me. I obediently take him, feeling myself growing wetter by the second.

"Good girl," he praises, and I just about fall apart.

Then, grabbing my hair tighter, he begins to pump harder and deeper. I gag, tears coming to my eyes as his cock hits the back of my throat, sliding deeper than any man has ever gone into me. I moan, grabbing his legs to steady me.

"Relax, sweetheart," he tells me, but doesn't let up. "Take it like a good girl."

I moan in affirmation, staring up at him, my expression one of desperation. Then he pumps harder. I squeal, feeling both more aroused and more uncomfortable than I've ever been. And despite how my body seemingly wants to reject what's happening, I can't help but desire more and more and more. The idea of me, half naked kneeling before this man while he has his way with me, fucking my mouth into submission, is just about the hottest thing that's ever happened to me.

And I desperately want it to never end.

I squeeze my eyes shut as more tears come to my eyes, moaning desperately as he continues to pump in and out of me, keeping a tight hold on my hair.

I hear him groaning quietly, and I open my eyes to see his jaw clenched, his eyes dark with desire. Suddenly he pulls out, and I gasp in shock as his cum sprays all over me neck and chest. Panting, I stare down at myself in shock, his liquid coating my chest, sliding down my breasts.

But Ezra wastes no time. Reaching down, he hooks his arms under my armpits, hoisting me back up onto the couch and then spreading my legs, kneeling between them. I stare down at him in shock.

He grins up at me, slowly sliding a hand up my thigh, pulling my dress with it. Once he reaches my waist, he snakes a finger under the band of my panties and slowly, tantalizingly pulls them down my legs, tossing them aside.

With one hand on each knee, he spreads me open, completely wide and bare before him. I feel myself redden at the sight of me—my black dress bunched around my waist, my pussy bare and exposed before him, my breasts on full display and covered in his own cum.

But he sure seems to love it.

He slides a finger along my inner thigh, causing my breath to quicken. When he reaches my slit, a deep moan escapes me, and I lean my head back against the couch cushions.

"Has it been hard not letting yourself find release this past week?" he asks me, sliding his finger up and down my slit.

I nod. "Yes," I whimper.

"Did you think about me, sweetheart?" he asks.

"Yes," I moan again.

"What did you think about?"

I blush harder.

"Tell me," he says, sliding a finger inside of me.

I gasp. "I—I thought about … about you touching me."

"Where?"

"There. Everywhere," I pant.

He starts slowly pumping his finger in and out of me. "You thought about me touching you even though you weren't allowed to make yourself come?" he says. "You poor thing."

I whine, bucking my hips toward him.

I hear him chuckle. I'd be angry at him for toying with me like this if I wasn't loving it so much. If I wasn't desperate for more.

"And what do you want now?" he presses.

I lean my head up to look into his eyes. He's smirking at me, his eyes alight with amusement. Fuck, he's enjoying this. Having me at his mercy. "I want you to make me come," I moan quietly.

"Can you beg for it, sweetheart?" he asks, inserting a second finger inside me, causing me to gasp in pleasure.

"Oh god, *please*," I whine, my breasts heaving with each breath. "I don't think I can take it anymore."

"You've been such a good girl," he says, pumping just a bit harder. "I suppose I could reward you."

Still pumping his fingers in and out of me, he lowers his head between my legs.

A shriek escapes me as his tongue finds my clit, and I know it won't take long for me to fall over the edge. He runs slow, deliberate circles around my clit, still fingering me. I grip the couch cushions beside me, gasping and moaning as he does his worst.

"Oh god," I cry as my climax nears. "Oh god, Ezra!" I shriek.

My orgasm tears through me, and I lie there, panting, as the waves continue to wash through me. Staring at the ceiling as the waves subside, it finally occurs to me what I've just done. Ezra and me.

There's no going back now.

Chapter 9

Ezra

I think this might be the most excited I've ever been to head to work on a Monday morning. I've been unable to keep my thoughts off of Emma all weekend. I had half a mind to call her on Saturday and have her come back over.

But I'd refrained. While I can tell she's obviously into what we're doing together, I don't quite know where her head is at when it comes to all this. Presumably she's just wanting something fun and casual. Which, so am I. At least, I think so.

Anyway, especially after our first time doing anything sexual, I wanted to give her some space to process. I don't want to smother her.

But now, as I walk down Newbury Street toward Bishop Jewelers, I feel actual goddamn *butterflies* in my stomach. Butterflies. Like I'm in high school or something.

Jesus Christ, I need to get a grip.

Sure, she's just about the most beautiful woman I've ever met. And she's smart and sweet and funny and ...

I shake my head. I was looking for a rebound and this is it. A rebound. Not ... something else.

I push open the door to Bishop Jewelers, immediately spying Emma behind the counter, which gets my heart rate up.

Her eyes meet mine, and a soft blush paints her cheeks. Fuck, I love it when she blushes. I especially love that I'm the one causing it. I shoot her a smile, glancing around to see that the store is empty. Rachel must not be in yet.

I stalk across the room, bracing my hands on the counter and leaning toward her. "How was your weekend?" I ask with a smirk.

She bites her lip. "It was good, Mr. Bishop."

Fuck, there she goes calling me *Mr. Bishop* again. I have half a mind to bend her over this counter and have her screaming that name over and over again.

The bell over the door rings, and I straighten up, turning to see Rachel entering. I look back to Emma. "Glad to hear it," I say with a professional smile, walking past her and into the back room.

I spend the day sneaking glances out my office door, catching glimpses of Emma when she happens to be in my line of sight. I stare at the outline of her curves through her blouse, remembering what it was like to see her naked breasts heaving as she'd moaned and whimpered my name.

Christ, I need to get it together or I'm not going to be able to get any work done today.

I resign myself to focus, although I still find myself doing a double take every time Emma walks by. At some point in the afternoon, I feel a presence in the doorway to my office, and I look up to see Emma.

She smiles shyly, and I wave her in.

"You miss me?" I tease.

She shrugs with a smirk.

I look past her, out onto the floor. Rachel seems busy with a customer.

"What're you working on in here?" she asks.

I shrug. "The typical. Emails, orders, the like. I also have to decide on some finalized new designs. I'm having a hard time making a choice."

Her eyebrow raises. "Designs for what?"

"Engagement rings. We try to release new designs every year—stay fresh and up to date with trends."

Her eyes widen slightly with interest. "Can I see them?" she asks.

I smile, beckoning her closer. "Sure."

She pulls a nearby chair close to mine, and I turn my computer toward her where an array of Jason's new ring designs are displayed. "Some of the more costly or difficult ones, like these," I say, pointing to one design in particular, "I've eliminated just because I don't think we can justify the markup on them. But I need to approve at least three of these remaining ones."

Emma leans in, taking a closer look. "They're all incredible," she says.

"I'm having a hard time deciding," I admit.

She cocks her head. "Well, I think you should pick at least one of these emerald cuts—it's what's trending right now in engagement ring design, so you know they'll sell well. And a classic princess cut is always going to do well." She pauses, thinking. "And as for the last one … just go with your gut. What feels right?"

I stare at her for a long moment. *What feels right?* What *does* feel right? Shit, I don't know anymore.

"Which one would you pick?" I ask her, breaking the silence.

She purses her lips. "Well, oval cuts are also kind of trending—"

"No." I shake my head. "Not what would you pick for the store. What would *you* pick? For yourself?"

She seems taken aback, and even I realize how suggestion it sounds. But I want to know. I truly do. I try to convince myself that it's because she's part of our target demographic—that her insight could be valuable, but if I'm honest with myself, that might not be the true reason.

She's quiet for a long moment, staring at the designs. Finally, she says, "This one." She points to one of Jason's more unique designs. A square bevel diamond with a gold band. "It feels … different," she says.

I smile. "It's settled then. The emerald, the princess, and the bevel."

She looks at me in surprise. "You're taking all my suggestions?"

"Of course. They're good suggestions. And now I can cross this off my list." I laugh.

She bites her lip to try and hold back her smile, and I can't help but grin at how damn cute it is. She stands to head back out onto the floor, but I grab her arm before she's able to go.

"This weekend," I say. "Are you busy?"

Her eyes sparkle. "Only with you," she says, and it makes my stomach do a fucking summersault.

"I have a cabin up in Maine. Come with me?"

She nods. "I can't wait."

Chapter 10

Emma

I wait patiently in my living room, my duffle packed and ready for the weekend ahead. I check the time on my phone—almost 6 o'clock. Ezra is sending a car to pick me up soon. A car that will take me to the airport, because apparently, we're *flying* to Ezra's cabin in Maine.

I almost laugh at the absurdity of it. I'm a New Englander, so of course I'm no stranger to weekend trips to the lake. But those trips usually entail a road trip packed with junk food, a crappy worn out cabin, and smores around a dilapidated fire.

Not private jets and a fancy luxury cabin right on the coast in Bar Harbor, Maine. But I suppose this is

Ezra's life. I'm just happy to be a part of it. At least for the weekend.

My phone buzzes—a text from Ezra's driver.

I grab my stuff and hurry out to the curb where a black SUV is waiting for me. I tentatively climb in. "For Emma, right?" I ask.

The man nods. "Yep. I'm taking you to the airport."

Instead of going to Boston Logan, like I'd assumed, we take a different route and end up at a completely different airport entirely. When I question the driver about this, he merely laughs. "Private jets don't fly out of Logan, Miss," he says.

Trying to hide my embarrassment, I just nod. Of course they don't.

The SUV pulls right up onto the tarmac, parking near a jet. I see Ezra standing on the stairs leading up to it, and he looks up as the car pulls in.

I hop out while the driver grabs my bag from the back, and Ezra smiles, walking up to pull me into a hug. I giggle against his chest. "I saw you like two hours ago at work."

"Yeah, way too long ago," he murmurs into my hair. I swat him playfully.

He grabs my bag from the driver, thanks him, and then takes my hand, leading me up the stairs and into the plane. While I know what private jets look like—mainly from movies—I've obviously never been on one. And seeing one in person, my mouth drops open. Instead of rows of bunched-up seats, there are couches and lounge chairs, with tables in between.

"How long is the flight?" I ask Ezra.

He shrugs. "Forty minutes?"

I shake my head. "I could spend the weekend *in here*," I say, gesturing around.

He comes up behind me, wrapping his arms around my waist and squeezing. "That could be arranged," he murmurs, making me giggle.

■■ ■ ■

We arrive in the coastal town of Bar Harbor, Maine approximately forty minutes later. And although Ezra and I didn't exactly join the mile high club, we definitely made it close.

Ezra has a car waiting for us when we land, which immediately takes us through the adorable town of Bar Harbor and then along some winding backroads until we come upon what I can only describe as a mansion located along one of the small island's gorgeous beaches.

I stare in awe as Ezra grabs our bags from the driver and then approaches the front door. He unlocks it and then turns back to me with a smirk. "You coming?"

I close my mouth and follow him, trying to keep my surprise in check. I really shouldn't be surprised. Of course Ezra Bishop owns an enormous beach house on an island in Maine.

The inside of the house is just as gorgeous as the outside. It's got an understated nautical theme going on, with white couches, light wood furnishings, and huge bay windows looking out to the ocean barely steps from the back door.

Ezra busies himself in the kitchen, pouring two glasses of wine and pulling something out of the fridge and popping it into the oven.

"What's that?" I ask.

He grins. "I had one of my private chefs mix something up and have it ready to go in the oven. It shouldn't take more than half an hour."

I try to conceal my shock. *One of* his private chefs? He has more than one? I almost laugh out loud. We make our way to the porch out back, the sound of the waves crashing and seagulls chirping the only noise to be heard.

I stand against the railing, as close to the ocean as I can get. I smile. I can't wait to explore the sand and beachcomb tomorrow. Ezra comes up behind me, wrapping his free arm around my waist and pulling me against him so he can press a kiss to my temple.

"It's beautiful here," I tell him.

He's quiet for a moment. "I always thought I'd bring my family here. *My family*—like, wife and kids stuff. I really thought it would happen until …"

I twist around so that I'm facing him, looking up into his eyes.

"Sorry." He shakes his head. "I don't mean to bring that up."

"No," I say, reaching up to rub my thumb over his cheek. "Don't be sorry." I search his eyes. "You know, it's not like that dream has to be over. You're not dead, Ezra," I say with a small laugh.

He chuckles, pulling me tighter against him. "No, I'm not dead," he says with a grin. He bites his lip, his brow furrowing as he stares into my eyes. "You're probably right. I don't need to throw that dream away entirely," he says slowly.

His eyes darken, and I feel my lower belly tightening. He leans down to press a kiss to my lips, soft at first, but quickly more and more demanding. I cling to the front of his shirt with my free hand, trying desperately not to spill my wine with the other.

Suddenly he pulls back, taking the glass from my hand and spinning around to place both our glasses on the table behind him. When he turns back to me, I reach for him, but he grasps my waist firmly, spinning me around and pinning me against the railing with his body.

I can already feel his arousal against my backside.

He presses his lips against my neck, his breath hot against my skin while he runs his hands over my breasts, my stomach, finding the hem of my t-shirt and lifting it. I gasp as he tugs the t-shirt up over my head and arms, tossing it aside.

I glance from side to side. The nearest house is quite a ways down the beach, but we're still technically out in the open.

"Sshhhh," Ezra murmurs against my ear, as if reading my thoughts. "No one's out here. And if they are, well … too bad." He nibbles my ear, causing me to moan softly.

He reaches up to cup my breasts, then he deftly finds the hooks at my back, undoing it and letting my breasts spill free. His hands are immediately on them as he squeezes and fondles them. I'm panting now, the wetness between my legs growing.

With one hand, he pinches my nipple—hard. I yelp, both in pain and pleasure.

He presses his lips against my ear. "You like that?" he asks.

I nod, surprising myself by the answer.

He pinches the other one, even harder, and I yelp.

Still squeezing and massaging a breast with one hand, he moves his other, lower, finding the waistband of my shorts and sliding a hand beneath them. Upon finding my wet center, he lets out a low growl.

"Fuck, Emma," he murmurs. "I love how wet you are for me."

I whine in response, pushing my backside up against him.

He slides a finger along my slit, up until he reaches my clit, and I cry out as he rubs slow circles around it.

"That's my girl," he says.

He pauses for a moment to grab the waistband of my shorts and underwear, pulling them both down in one stroke, leaving me completely and utterly naked, pinned against the railing.

"Emma," he says slowly, and I about fall apart at the way he says my name. He continues to rub slow circles around my clit. "Are you on anything?"

I immediately know what he's talking about. "I have an IUD," I say quickly.

"So you're okay without a condom?"

I nod.

"Good. I like the idea of filling you with my cum."

My mouth drops open at his dirty words, my core heating up even more.

I feel Ezra step back slightly, and I look over my shoulder to see him unzipping his jeans. While I can't quite see his cock from here, I remember the size of it from when I'd taken him in my mouth, and I feel a bundle of nerves growing in my stomach. Will it … hurt?

He presses up against me again, and I can feel the tip of him at my entrance. I stiffen, suddenly nervous, but once his hands are back on me, my breasts, my clit, I feel myself relax just a bit.

"Are you ready for me, sweetheart?" he breathes against my ear.

I nod. "Yes."

Then he enters me. I gasp at the overwhelming sensation of being stretched wider than I ever have. I grip the railing, feeling overwhelming pleasure and a tinge of pain.

"Shhhh," Ezra breathes against my ear, seemingly sensing my discomfort. "That's my good girl." His words seem to open me up, taking all of him in.

He pauses for a moment, his cock fully inside of me. He runs his hands over my breasts, down my body, to my clit. I bite my lip, moaning softly.

Then he starts pumping. Slowly at first, but then faster. I grip the railing for support, leaning forward, my breasts dangling beneath me as he thrusts harder and faster. He reaches down to fondle them, plucking at and pinching my nipples as he fucks me.

I cry out with each thrust, feeling as though I might split apart at the seams. The pleasure is blinding, overwhelming. Sounds I didn't know I was capable of making are coming out of my mouth, and I'm sure if his neighbors are home, they can hear everything.

"You're such a good girl," Ezra praises as he fucks me harder. "Taking all me like this."

I moan in reply, hanging onto the railing for dear life.

He snakes a hand between my legs, finding my clit and rubbing.

I scream, seeing stars. I imagine the sight of myself, completely naked, being fucked over a railing by a fully clothed man, my breasts jostling below me.

"Ezra, I'm going to come," I cry, my mouth open in a permanent shriek.

"Good," he pants, somehow thrusting into me harder.

I feel my orgasm crash through me, tearing me apart from the inside out. I melt into the railing, gasping for breath as Ezra continues to pump, finally finishing and stilling inside of me. We stay there, panting, for a few moments, before he finally pulls out and steps back.

I twirl around, covering my breasts and suddenly remembering how exposed we are. I can already feel his cum dripping down my inner thighs.

He smirks down at me, taking me in. I blush. "Let's go get you cleaned up," he says.

Chapter 11

Ezra

I stare at Emma's sleeping form beside me, too awake to go back to sleep, but much too content to get up and start my day. So instead, I simply lie beside her, propped up on my elbow, gazing at her as her chest softly rises and falls.

It's so strange to be back at this beach house. The last time I'd been here was with Diane for one of our anniversaries. I can't even remember which one it was. It was probably two or more years ago. And even then, things had felt strained.

It's funny, though. Even though thinking of her still brings out some sadness, hurt, betrayal, it doesn't sting as much as it did. All of those bitter emotions are softened by the woman lying next to me. The woman who, last night, I'd been fantasizing about having kids with—those said kids running around this house, playing in the waves out back, making sandcastles on the beach.

Shit. This whole rebound idea is working out terribly. I smirk slightly. The only problem is that I'm still not sure how Emma feels. She's obviously into me. But she's young and gorgeous, with her whole life ahead of her. She might not be looking for someone to settle down with. And I can hardly blame her.

Emma rolls over, pulling me from my thoughts. She opens her eyes, her gaze landing sleepily on mine. She smiles in surprise. "Hi." Her voice is thick and groggy, and it makes me want to wrap her up in my arms and smother her with kisses.

"Morning, sweetheart," I say, reaching out to brush a strand of hair from her face.

She stretches lazily. I lean down to press a kiss to her forehead.

"Coffee," she murmurs, her eyes closed.

I laugh, taking her hand and pulling her up. "In the kitchen. Let's go."

Smiling, she grabs an old sweater of mine lying on the chair in the corner, wrapping it around herself and then following me out of the bedroom and down the hallway to the kitchen. My sweater is long enough that it goes halfway down her thighs, completely enveloping her pajama shorts. Fuck, she looks adorable in it.

I quickly brew a pot of coffee, making two cups for us in between smothering Emma with hugs and kisses.

Our mugs of hot coffee warm in our hands, we carry them out to the back porch where we settle into wicker chairs. I stare out at the ocean waves crashing nearby, the sound like a lullaby. The cool breeze feels soft against my skin, and I glance sideways at Emma.

She's smiling at me. I raise an eyebrow in question. "What are you thinking about?"

Almost as if she didn't realize she'd been staring at me, she quickly shakes her head. "Oh, nothing."

"Tell me," I insist, grinning.

She bites her lip in thought. "I've just never … never had anyone treat me like this." She takes a breath. "Not the whole private jet, mansion on the ocean thing," she clarifies with a laugh. "But just … caring. So attentive, making me laugh, making me coffee." She meets my gaze. "You're so sweet to me."

As much as what she said should bring a smile to my lips, it doesn't. I stare back at her, my brow furrowing, caught on one word in particular. *Never.* This gorgeous, lovely, sweet woman has never had anyone treat her like this? The idea just about breaks my heart.

She seems to sense my discomfort, and she frowns as well. "What?"

I reach for her hand, running my thumb over her palm. "It makes me sad that I'm the first to have treated you well," I say simply.

As if just now realizing the reality of what she'd admitted, she nods slowly. Then she shrugs. "I guess I haven't been lucky when it comes to guys."

I sigh. *Well, that's over now.* The thought comes to my mind so quickly that it almost slips right past my lips. I suppress my shock and squeeze her hand. "I guess I haven't been lucky with women either," I admit with a humorless grin. "Until now."

She stares at me for a long moment, finally leaning over to press her soft lips against mine. My cock stirs in my pants. God, I haven't been this hot for a woman since I was a teenager.

We slowly finish our coffees, staring out at the morning sun glistening over the ocean.

"I should probably get dressed," Emma says eventually, standing from her chair and heading inside. I take our mugs to the sink in the kitchen and then follow her into the bedroom where she's rifling through her duffle bag.

I come up behind her, wrapping my arms around her waist and pulling her against me. "I think before you get all dressed up, I might want to see you *undressed*," I say, to which she giggles.

"Oh yeah?" She twirls around, pressing her hands against my chest, reaching up to softly kiss me. She pulls back. "But this time ..." She tugs at my t-shirt. "I want all this gone. You've seen all of me, and I haven't seen all of you yet."

I grin. She's right. I hadn't even realized that both of our encounters included her completely naked while I remained mostly clothed. "What did I originally say about who's in charge when it comes to the bedroom?" I murmur, taking her chin in my hand and tilting her head up toward me. Her breath catches in her throat, and I feel myself stiffening. I smirk. "But I suppose that's a fair request."

I step back, grabbing the hem of my t-shirt and lifting it over my head and then tossing it aside.

Emma bites her lip as she takes in my torso, desire evident in her gaze.

"Your turn," I say, gesturing to her pajama top.

She does as I ask, pulling her top over her head and tossing it to the floor, revealing those perfect breasts again. Her pink nipples are already stiff peaks.

I slip my fingers under the waistband of my sleep shorts and boxers, letting them fall to the floor and then stepping out of them. I wouldn't normally be this hard this quickly, but something about Emma has my cock stiff and erect, ready for whatever comes. Her eyes widen as she takes it in. I know my size is larger than normal, and this reaction isn't exactly unusual, although it's been a while since I was in any kind of new relationship.

I gesture to her pajama bottoms, and she quickly strips them and her panties, leaving both of us completely bare before each other. We stand there for a few heartbeats, taking each other in. Then I stalk toward her, leaning down to scoop her up into my arms and then depositing her on the bed. She yelps in surprise, but I'm already climbing over top of her, grabbing both of her wrists and pinning them above her head. She gasps in shock, her breasts heaving as she pants, staring up at me with wide eyes.

I grin down at her. I reach over the side of the bed, to my bag on the floor where I retrieve the tie I'd been wearing yesterday. Emma watches with wide eyes as I gently tie it around her wrists, fastening the end of it to the headboard. Tight enough to hold her in place, but loose enough to break free if she really wanted to. Her mouth opens in shock.

I raise an eyebrow in question. "Is this okay?" I ask her seriously.

She nods immediately, her eyes darkening in desire. Fuck, it's taking everything within me not to fuck her brains out right now. But I want this to be slow and deliberate. I have a plan.

I sit up, gazing down at her perfect body, her wrists tied above her head. I reach out to run my thumb over her bottom lip, then down her neck, her chest, in between her breasts, then drawing lazily circles on her stomach.

With a hand on each knee, I spread her legs, settling myself between them. I lower my head, my eyes still pinned on hers. "I'm gonna make you feel so good, sweetheart," I murmur, leaning farther to run my tongue along her already slick opening.

She gasps and bucks her hips. I chuckle. "Be still like a good girl," I demand before returning to her center. I take my sweet time running my tongue along her slit, up to her clit, and back down again. Soon she's panting and moaning, and I have to hold her hips down in order to keep her still, my fingers digging into the soft flesh of her hips. I run my tongue over her clit, faster and faster, and I can hear her breathing quicken. Her moans become more and more frantic, and I can tell she's close to coming. But just as she's about to orgasm, I pull back.

She gasps in surprise. "I didn't—"

"I know you didn't," I say with a smirk.

Understanding dawns on her, and she sucks in a desperate breath of air.

I crawl up her body, pressing a soft kiss to the tip of her right breast. "You'll come when I want you to come," I tell her, kissing her left breast. She moans quietly.

I draw lazy circles around her nipple with my tongue, and then I pull it into my mouth completely, sucking. She arches her back, throwing her head back against the bed.

After a few moments of sucking on her breasts, I move back between her legs, this time inserting a few fingers inside of her as I lick her clit. She bucks her hips, pulling on her restraints, writhing in torturous ecstasy as I pleasure her.

"*Ezra*," she moans. "I'm so close."

I pull back, and she lets out a frustrated cry, writhing and pulling against the bedframe.

Just the sight of her has me aroused enough to fucking come.

I reach up to run my thumbs over her nipples, creating slow, soft circles. She lets out what can only be described as a sob.

"What do you want, sweetheart?" I ask her.

"Please," she whines, arching her back and bucking her hips. "Please let me come."

"But I'm having so much fun watching you squirm," I say, pinching her nipples.

She cries out, shaking her head back and forth.

"I could do this all day."

"Ezra!" she cries as I return to her clit, rubbing slow circles. "I can't take it, *please*."

"Oh, you can take it," I assure her, working her up to an almost-orgasm again before pulling away.

She cries out, writhing so much that I have to pin her down. "I need you inside me," she pants. "*Please*."

I had intended on torturing her for much longer, but her pleas have me almost bursting, and I don't think *I* can wait much longer.

"Yeah?" I press, crawling up her body and settling myself between her welcoming thighs. She wraps her legs around me, practically pulling me against her. "You want my thick cock filling you up?"

She nods, panting desperately.

"Say it," I order.

"I want your cock inside of me," she breathes.

At that, I slam the length of myself into her, and she gasps. I begin thrusting hard and fast, her breasts jostling with each thrust, her wrists straining against the fabric of my tie.

Her cries become louder and louder, filling the room.

I brace myself on either side of her, pumping faster and faster. Fuck, I'm not going to last long at all. I can already tell.

She screams, and I feel her pussy pulsing around my cock as her orgasm floods through her. At that, I let myself go, releasing myself inside of her.

I collapse on top her, reaching up to quickly untie her restraints. She pulls her arms down, wrapping them around me, and we lie like that, panting, for what feels like hours. And in the glow of the aftermath, a startling realization settles over me. Something I'd considered a possibility but that I now know to be a fact.

That Emma Hayes is far from a rebound. That she will either heal my broken heart or shatter it forever.

Chapter 12

Emma

I return home Sunday night absolutely giddy. After spending the weekend walking the beaches of Maine, exploring the quaint town of Bar Harbor, and letting Ezra do just about the filthiest things I've ever allowed someone to do to me, my brain is an oxytocin-infused blur.

And what's worse is that even though we've been apart for approximately four hours, I can't wait to see him again. I almost laugh at the absurdity. I'm like some giddy highschooler.

But that giddiness dries up in an instant when I hear a knock at the door and glance through the peephole to see who it is.

Shit.

I unlock the door, and Justin barges in, shutting the door behind him. "What are you doing here?" I demand.

"Where have you been all weekend?" he shoots back.

"I—I've been with … Ezra," I admit.

He nods. "So I'm guessing you've finally fucked, yeah?"

I feel myself redden, and all of a sudden this weekend spent with Ezra, all our moments together, feel cheap and horrible and slimy. God, what had I even been thinking? That I could somehow untangle myself from this mess and that Ezra and I had any sort of chance at … anything?

"I'll take that as a yes," Justin says derisively. "Okay, then we'll have to set up some kind of situation where I can catch you in the act, get pictures, and leak them to the press."

My eyes widen. "Pictures?"

He rolls his eyes. "Nothing dirty, just you two out at a bar or something. You'll need to kiss, but nothing sexual."

I'm silent, realizing I hadn't really thought this far into the plan. I'd been so blinded by the fear of my videos being leaked that nothing else had mattered.

Justin seems to notice my discomfort. "Better a photo of you kissing Ezra plastered over the local newspapers than a video of me fucking you plastered all over the internet." He pins me with a hard stare. "Right?"

I swallow. "Justin," I say after a long pause. "Why does this matter so much to you?"

He shakes his head, opening his mouth to refute me, but I beat him to it.

"Just let it go. Please. You don't have to do this— any of this."

"We're doing it, Emma. Get over it," he snaps, taking a step toward me, towering over me.

"Please," I beg, feeling myself near tears. "This won't affect his company, nothing will. Besides, there's barely a scandal to be had, he's ..." I falter for a moment. "He's divorcing his wife anyway."

At this, Justin raises an eyebrow. He seems to ponder this for a moment, but then he doubles down. "All the more reason to leak this scandal before his divorce goes public."

I stare at him incredulously.

"Make plans to meet him somewhere public, somewhere I can also be. Let me know the time and location—and remember to kiss him, feel him up, be romantic. It needs to be obvious in the picture." He turns to go, but I reach for his arm.

99

"Justin, *please*," I beg. "Please don't make me do this."

He glares at me. "It's this or those pictures, Em." His tone is icy. He continues on his way to the door, but I grab his arm, pulling with all my might. "Let go," he snaps, but I don't.

"Please," I say, my voice coming out through a broken sob.

"Jesus Christ, Emma, just fucking do it!" he yells, grabbing me by the shoulders and slamming me into the wall.

My head makes contact with the drywall, an immediate ringing taking center stage in my ears. I cry out in pain, sliding to the floor while Justin steps back. He stares down at me for a long moment, although I can barely make him out through blurry vision. After a few seconds, he leaves, slamming the door behind him.

In the silence, surrounded by pain, ringing, and distress, I give in to the sobs.

Chapter 13

Emma

Gripping my purse in my hand, I step out of the Uber in front of Ezra's Beacon Hill townhouse. I'd spent last night crying and therefore, this morning, trying to depuff my eyes. The side of my face, just above my eyebrow is sporting a nasty, purple bruise from where Justin had slammed me into the wall. I'd slathered it with concealer and had done a convincing job of hiding it. At least nobody at work had noticed.

I'd spent the day with a knot in my stomach that had lessened slightly when I'd gotten a text from Ezra asking me to come over to his place for dinner tonight. Despite the stress of everything going on around me, the idea of seeing him sends a wave of calm over me. Like, somehow, we could get through this together.

Even though, deep down, I know the only way out of this is through. Part of me wants to come clean, to tell him what's been going on and simply let the cards fall as they may. But the image of that video Justin has looms over me.

My life would be absolutely ruined.

I walk up the steps to Ezra's apartment and ring the doorbell. He buzzes me in, and I make my way up to the top floor like the last time I was here. When the elevator doors ding open and I see Ezra standing in his kitchen with a blue apron tied around his waist, the pit in my stomach vanishes.

A smile spreads across my face when his gaze meets mine.

"There's my sunshine," he says with a grin, placing a spatula on the counter and striding toward me to pull me against his chest. It's so warm and comforting there, I feel like I might almost cry.

And that's when it hits me.

I have to tell him.

The knot in my stomach is back, and Ezra turns away from me, back to the kitchen, unaware of my sudden shift in energy. I swallow, staring ahead. I don't know how I thought I could get away with any of this. How any of this would have turned out alright.

But regardless of what happens with Justin and the video, I have to come clean. Ezra doesn't deserve whatever Justin has up his sleeve. And I sure as hell won't help him accomplish it. And it's more than that.

After this last weekend …

Ezra is more to me than my hot boss. A fun time. He's—

But I shake my head, afraid to put it to words. Because what if I tell him everything and he wants nothing to do with me? It's definitely plausible.

"How was your day?" Ezra calls, pulling me from my thoughts.

I blink a few times, following him into the kitchen and forcing a smile on my face. "Good. Just normal work stuff."

He nods, stirring what looks to be a pot of spaghetti noodles on the stove. He glances over his shoulder, staring at me for a long moment. "You okay?"

I nod, trying to keep up the happy façade. "Yeah, just tired."

He leaves the stove, coming around the side of the counter to where I'm sitting on a stool. He leans down to press his lips against mine, kissing me softly. I lean into him, my eyes fluttering closed. After a long moment, he pulls back, looking down at me with a grin.

But then slowly, his brow furrows, and his gaze leaves mine. "What is this?" he asks, reaching out a hand to my cheek.

My eyes widen. I glance sideways to the mirror on the wall across from me. Fuck. The makeup I'd meticulously doused my face in this morning as worn off slightly, showing just enough purple to look strange.

Ezra licks his thumb, reaching out to swipe it across my cheekbone. His eyes widen, and I can only assume that the bruise is now perfectly visible. Probably even darker than it was this morning.

His mouth opens in shock. "Is this from this weekend? Did I ..." Horror washes over his features, and he reaches out to gently cup my face. "Jesus, *Emma*."

While we'd done a few rough things in bed, it definitely wasn't rough enough to leave any bruises. I shake my head, opening my mouth.

"Christ," he says, cradling my head as if it's so fragile it could break, his expression one of pure and absolute remorse.

"No, no!" I cry, reaching up to place my hand over his. "It wasn't you," I tell him, feeling a soft lump rising in my throat. I try to swallow it down, but it's stubborn. "I—" I begin, but I choke on my words.

Ezra's horrified expression turns to one of concern, and he crouches before me. "What happened?" he asks.

I bite my lip, unable to stop the flow of tears. "It … I—I have something to tell you," I choke out.

He waits patiently, his forehead creased in concern.

I try to meet his gaze but find that I'm too ashamed to. "My ex, the one I told you about—"

"*He* did this?" Ezra asks, his jaw tightening.

I nod, feeling more tears fall from my eyes. "He came over to my apartment because—because …" I stutter. "His parents jewelry business was shut down, he blames it on Bishop Jewelers, and he wanted to get back at you—lash out. He told me to seduce you, that it would ruin your reputation. And I agreed because …" I take in a shaky breath. "He has videos of me—of us, doing …" A sob escapes my throat. "He threatened to leak the videos everywhere if I didn't do what he said."

Ezra straightens slowly, his hands leaving me and falling to his sides. I stare up at him. While his eyebrows are still scrunched in concern, there's a new emotion there. Disappointment, sadness, hurt. At *me*. I almost want him to be angry. To yell at me, to be furious. His anger would be easier to take than this. Than this devastation I see in his eyes.

"I'm so sorry, Ezra," I cry, wiping the tears from my eyes. "I never wanted to hurt you, but I couldn't let him share those videos—I just couldn't. And as we got to know each other, my feelings were real—they *are* real."

He looks away, unable to meet my gaze. I reach for him, but he holds up a hand, stopping me. "It's fine," he says, but it's short, and it cuts me to the bone.

I swallow, trying to compose myself.

He looks back at me, staring me down for a long moment. "What's his name?" he asks me.

"Justin?"

"His full name," he clarifies, his expression hard.

"Justin Stoll," I say quietly.

He nods. "Where does he live?"

I frown. "Why?"

"Where does he live, Emma?" he asks me, his voice dangerously low.

I swallow, hastily mumbling his address.

He turns, pulling off the apron he's wearing and tossing it on the counter. He grabs his wallet from the entryway table, stuffing it into his pocket.

I get up. "What are you doing?"

He doesn't answer me, simply kneels down to hurriedly slide on his shoes. He stands, giving me one last, hard stare. "It'd probably be best if you weren't here when I get back," he says quietly, and it just about breaks my heart.

And with that, he turns on his heel and leaves the apartment.

Chapter 14

Ezra

I grip the steering wheel as if somehow strangling it hard enough will relieve the torrent of emotions welling up inside of me. The GPS on my phone gives me directions, and I follow them.

I keep having flashes of this past weekend in my mind. Emma and I holding hands, talking, having sex—the feelings that had emerged, the clarity I'd felt. That Emma was more to me than just a fling, that Emma was someone I could have something real with. I'd already made plans, gone over things in my head, fantasized about where it all could have gone.

And then this.

What was wrong with me? I should've known better than to let myself fall like this.

I slam my hand against the steering wheel. "Fuck!" I yell, but it doesn't quell the hurt as much as I'd wanted it to. It still sits there, heavy in the pit of my stomach, like it might sit there forever.

I pull up in front of Justin Stoll's apartment complex, slamming the car into park and storming up the front steps.

Because regardless of how betrayed I feel by Emma right now, the burning devastation coursing through my veins, I can't stop thinking about that gnarly purple bruise on her cheekbone. How it had spread up along her temple, over her eyebrow. My hands clench into fists thinking about how that had come to happen. Had he hit her? Thrown her against something?

I reach Justin's apartment, and I bang on the door. When he doesn't immediately answer, I bang again. And again and again until he opens it, a confused and irritated look on his face.

"What do you—"

I push past him, into the apartment, slamming the door behind me. He stumbles backward. He's a scrawny kid, shorter than me too. He stares up at me for a moment, and then I see what looks to be recognition dawning on his features. He knows who I am.

Good. He'd better.

He holds up his hands, obviously taking in my anger. "Look, I don't know why you're here, but—"

"You hit her?" I growl, my jaw tight, my fists clenched.

I see what looks to be fear flash through his eyes, but he quickly hides it. He shakes his head. "No, I didn't hit anyone."

"Then what'd you do?" I ask, stalking toward him. "Throw her into something?"

He backs up, shaking his head.

"She didn't get that bruise in her sleep," I snap as his back hits the wall behind him.

He holds up his hands. "It was an accident, man, it was nothing."

I reach out and grip the collar of his shirt, yanking him toward me. "You pathetic fuck," I spit.

He pushes against my chest, but I slam his back against the wall. His eyes widen in fear, and he holds up his hands. "Look, I'm sorry, okay? It was an accident, I swear."

He shove him away from me, afraid I might lost control and punch him in the face if I don't cool down. He stumbles back.

"Stay away from her," I demand. "And don't even think about posting those disgusting videos you have of her, either."

Justin straightens, raising in eyebrow in surprise. "Oh, so you know about all that, huh?"

I grit my teeth.

"I guess she told you everything."

I don't respond.

He shakes his head, standing straighter, trying to regain what's left of his dignity. "That deal is between me and Emma."

I cock my head, my glare deepening. He can't be serious right now.

"She does what I ask of her, and I hold up my end of the bargain—not releasing the video."

My fists clench at my sides. He better start saying something else, or I might end up clobbering him to the floor right here in his living room.

"Although I hear there might already be something scandalous that the press could hear about?" he purrs.

I frown, staring him down. But the longer I stare at him, the surer I become. He knows. He fucking knows about Diane and the cheating. Probably through Emma. Although based on that bruise on the side of her face, I don't blame her for spilling what she knew. This guy is a fucking psychopath.

Justin shrugs. "All I want is the Bishop name sullied. I want you to pay at least *something* for what you did to my family's business."

"I don't even know what business your family had," I say in exasperation.

"Well, it went under because of Bishop Jewelers!" Justin shoots back.

I roll my eyes. It doesn't matter. Reasoning with him isn't going to do anything.

Justin crosses his arms. "I don't know, maybe a scandal about you and your wife splitting is enough for me to not ruin poor Emma's honor."

I stare at him for a long moment. Finally, I break the silence. "There will be a story about my divorce within the week. You don't leak the video, now or ever. Delete it. And …" I cross the room, moving to stand within a foot of him, towering over his much shorter frame. "You ever so much as lay eyes on Emma again, I will personally hunt you down and beat you into the floor. You understand?"

Justin nods, trying to keep up a sly façade—but I can see the fear in his eyes.

"Good." I back up, throwing him one last dirty look before turning and exiting the apartment, slamming the door on my way out.

I sit in my car in the dark for what feels like hours, a million thoughts running through my mind. Diane, her new lover, Justin, Bishop Jewelers, Emma, everything. A twinge of guilt runs through me, thinking about what I'm about to do.

But the more I think about it, the more I realize that, in all honesty, Diane had it coming. There was no way we'd be able to keep the story of her cheating quiet forever. I hoped we could get away with it, but I know now that that was naïve. And why do I keep feeling the need to protect her? She broke my heart. She left me. And cruelly, too.

No. I don't wish her the worst, but I also can't protect her from the consequences of her own actions. And it's time I start acting in my own interests. I'll make sure she gets her fair share in the divorce, but I'm not going to lie about why that divorce came about.

Besides, doing this will save Emma from the humiliation and possible ruin of having intimate videos of her leaked online. As much as I want to hate her for what she's done, I can't ignore the fact that she was desperate, forced into a corner.

I shake my head, pulling up my phone.

It's well past working hours, but I pay my lawyer enough that he'll answer my calls no matter the hour. I click his contact and wait for him to answer.

Chapter 15

Emma

After leaving Ezra's apartment, I go home and cry myself to sleep, filled with guilt and self-loathing. When he doesn't come to the office the next day—his normal day in—the guilt continues to grow. After two days of no contact, I send him a text.

No answer.

By Thursday, the sick feeling in the pit of my stomach is becoming a familiar presence.

I can only assume that whatever relationship we'd had is over. I'd partially assumed my job was as well, but when Ezra didn't come in Monday to fire me, I'm beginning to wonder if maybe he won't. I think back to our earlier conversation—how he'd said my job was safe no matter what happened. But he can't include my literal betrayal in that, can he? If so, it would be beyond any mercy I deserve.

I'm also dying to know what happened after he'd stormed out of his apartment Monday night. Surely he'd gone to see Justin, right? And now that I think about it, I haven't heard from Justin either. No texts asking how the plan is going, no pushing to institute our deal. It makes me nervous. Is he going to leak that video after all?

I push the door open, stepping into Bishop Jewelers, the bell above me dinging softly. Rachel looks up when she sees me and immediately purses her lips. "You sure you're not coming down with something? I swear you've seemed ill all week."

I shake my head. "Allergies," I lie. That would explain the eyes puffy from crying all night.

She shakes her head like she doesn't believe me, looking back down at her phone. "Did you hear the news?" she says without looking up.

"What news?" I ask, not really caring. I tuck my purse into the back room and come out to join her by the front counter.

She turns to me, eyes wide. "You haven't heard?"

"Heard what?"

She turns her phone toward me, and I lean in. On it is a display from a Boston local news site. All I catch is the name "Ezra," and I immediately grab the phone from her.

Engagement Ring Mogul Dethroned in Cheating Scandal.

I widen my eyes. "Shit," I breathe, skimming the article.

"Yeah," Rachel agrees. "Can you believe she cheated on him?"

My mouth opens wide in shock as I continue the article. Cheating scandal. But they're talking about *Diane*, not me. Ezra's wife. Well, ex-wife, I suppose.

"It's awful," Rachel continues. "He's such a sweet guy."

I look through the rest of the article. Apparently, he served her papers on Tuesday. She didn't see it coming, despite already living with her lover. It goes on to rehash Ezra and Diane's fairytale love story from a decade ago, tearing it apart bit by bit, calling it a sham to sell more engagement rings. Because how could a real true love end like this?

I hand the phone back to Rachel, unable to read more. Suddenly, a thought occurs to me. "Will this affect business, you think?" I ask her.

Rachel scoffs. "No. If anything, it's publicity. And you know what they say—all press is good press."

116

She chuckles, then becomes serious again. "No, Bishop Jewelers is fine. It just kinda sucks for Ezra, I imagine." She scrunches up her face, turning to begin unpacking a new delivery.

I remain standing where I am, still shell shocked. And through the haze, another thought hits me. With Diane's cheating hitting the news, soiling the Bishop name … does that mean I'm off the hook with Justin? Surely any scandal I could drum up would pale in comparison to this. There's no more harm to be done.

I almost want to text him and ask, but I'm afraid that reaching out to him will do more harm than good. I suppose I'll just have to wait around and see if that horrid video shows up on my socials. I shudder at the thought.

My mind wanders back to Ezra. What Rachel said was right. Bishop Jewelers won't suffer from this. Only Ezra. My heart breaks just thinking about it. And it breaks even more knowing about the part I played in all this. Biting back the lump forming in my throat, I vow to stay as much out of his way as possible, get through working here until I can find another job. He deserves better. A life without me in it, reminding him of the terrible things I did.

"Ooooh, Emma," Rachel calls from the other side of the store. "Come look at these." She has a delivery package open on the counter, a few smaller boxes scattered about that she'd obviously taken out.

Trying to shake the emotions from my mind, I hurry over to her side. On the counter, each in their own plush velvet box, are a handful of engagement rings. I raise an eyebrow, unsure why this attention is warranted. Our store is filled to the brim with engagement rings.

"These are the new prototype designs from Jason," Rachel explains, reaching for one of them. She pulls it from the box, sliding it on her finger. She holds it out, tilting her head and observing it. "Ugh, I want an emerald cut so badly. If only I can find a man first." She giggles.

I glance over the others, and one in particular catches my eye. My heart lurches, remembering the sweet moment in his office that Ezra and I had shared. I reach for the ring, holding it gently. It's the gold bezel ring I'd picked out. The one I'd said I'd want for myself.

I stare down at it sadly.

I'm about to set it back down on the counter, when another element snags my attention. Not the ring, but the box. I turn it slightly so I can see the top of it. Now that I notice, I see all the ring boxes have some kind of sticker on the front—like something made with a label maker.

My breath catches in my throat when I see what it says.

Emma.

I stare down at it, feeling a tear coming to my eye. He'd named the ring after me.

I snap the box shut, putting it down before Rachel notices my reaction. Hopefully she won't notice the name, and if she does, mine is a common enough name for it to not raise suspicion. At least I hope so.

Walking away to compose myself, I decide to make an amendment to my earlier vow. If, in the end, Ezra truly wants nothing to do with me, I'll give it to him. I'll honor it. But not without at least pleading my case. Not without trying. Because Ezra Bishop is too good a man to give up.

And I'm not giving him up without a fight.

Chapter 16

Emma

I park outside Ezra's townhouse, sitting in the dark silence for a long moment. The sun has long since set, and I stare up at the lights through his windows. I savor the moment for a few heartbeats. Because after I go in and speak with him, after I bare my soul and see what he says—that's that. He'll either forgive me or he won't.

And this, right now—the hope—might just be the best I'll ever get.

Because in all honesty, I don't expect forgiveness. If I were in his situation, I can't say I'd be so easy to forgive. I truly can't blame him. And that makes it all the harder.

With one last deep breath, I grab my purse from the passenger seat and hop out of the car. I ring his doorbell, smoothing my hair nervously. I know he has cameras down here. He'll immediately know it's me.

Suddenly, it occurs to me that he might not even let me in. But I don't have much time to dwell on that thought before I hear the familiar buzz of his front door unlocking.

Surprised, because he hadn't greeted me over the intercom, I hesitantly push the door open and step inside. I glance around the large lobby, realizing I really haven't explored much of his house. All our time had been spent on his top two floors.

I shift uncomfortably, having no idea where he could be in this enormous townhouse. But then I hear the sound of a door opening and closing, and then, around the corner, strides Ezra.

He's wearing sweatpants and a dark green t-shirt—and fuck, if he doesn't somehow look sexier in that than he does in his everyday suits.

He comes to stand before me, silent, farther apart than we'd normally stand. His hands are in his pockets as he surveys me with a look of, not anger as I'd expected, but simple sadness.

"Hi," I greet quietly, my voice catching on the word.

He offers me a tight-lipped grin that doesn't reach his eyes. "Hi."

I shuffle anxiously. "Can we talk?"

He shrugs. "I let you in."

Right. I nod, adrenaline coursing through me. "I saw the news. About you and your ... wife."

"Ex-wife," he clarifies quickly.

I nod. "I'm sorry it's all so ... negative."

He's silent for a long moment. Long enough that I worry he's not going to respond at all. "It was meant to be negative," he finally says.

I frown in confusion, unsure what he means. I open my mouth to question him, but he beats me to it.

"I spoke with Justin."

My eyes widen at that. "Spoke?" I repeat. "Only spoke?" I'd been afraid their confrontation wouldn't include much speaking.

He noticeably grits his jaw at that. "Basically." He lets out an irritated sigh. "You won't have to worry about that video of yours showing up anywhere," he says, leveling me with a sincere stare. "It was a trade. That story in the press about Diane cheating? It was enough for him to drop whatever deal he'd made with you."

I stare at him, dumbfounded, for a long moment. "You leaked it to the press?" I put together.

He nods, lips still pursed. "And I had my lawyer send Justin a letter threatening a lawsuit if those videos ever see the light of day, outlining the fact that I have *unlimited* resources when it comes to waging a legal war with him. If that's not persuading enough, I don't know what is. He's also got a restraining order on him—he can't come within a hundred feet of you."

I take the information as it comes at me, my disbelief growing with every second. "You'd ... do that for me?" I finally say, my voice barely above a whisper.

He shrugs, not meeting my eyes. "The news about Diane would've leaked at some point. And—" his eyes meet mine "—the idea of that fucker hurting you ..." His hands clench at his sides, and he shakes his head.

"But you did it. You did all that for *me*. After ..." I stare at him, my heart breaking even further. That even after I'd hurt this man, he'd gone to war for me. He'd saved my life, defended me against Justin, thrown his reputation to the wolves all for ... what? Me? Just *me*?

"Ezra," I whisper, my voice catching. "I'm so sorry." I shake my head, the guilt boiling over. "I never meant to hurt you, I was just blinded by the fear of what Justin could do. I shouldn't have agreed, and I shouldn't have played with you. It was awful of me

123

and unforgiveable—regardless of what Justin threatened me with." I wrap my arms around my waist, hugging myself for comfort. "I never thought it would get this far, I never thought I'd fall …" I swallow, realizing as the words slip out how real they are. "… in love with you."

At this, Ezra's eyes widen slightly. "You love me?" he repeats. It's the first time I've seen him not composed, not fully in control. He truly looks shocked, incredulous, and … something else I can't quite identify.

I nod. I bite my lip, suddenly feeling stupid, silly. I hadn't even fully realized the extent of my feelings for him until this very moment. But the more I sit in it, the more I realize how true it is. I'm in love with Ezra Bishop, as implausible as that seems. And as the seconds tick by without a response, my heart feels like it might explode.

Ezra stares at me for a long moment. A long, torturous moment. "I didn't think I could ever really love again after Diane," he says softly. "I never thought I'd feel that way again." He walks toward me. "Until you," he breathes, looking down at me.

My breath hitches in my throat, and I stare up at him.

He reaches down to cup my face in his hands. "I love you, Emma Hayes. And I don't care what you did—all I care about is that you love me back." And with that, he crushes his lips against mine, wrapping his arms around my body and pulling me against him.

I melt into him, my mind going a thousand different places at once. Shock, relief, joy, but most of all—desire. I cling to him, grasping the fabric of his shirt and pulling him against me.

Without breaking our kiss, he reaches down with both hands to grip my ass, hoisting me up and urging me to wrap my legs around his waist. I do, and he carries me down the hallway and through a door. I break our kiss to look around long enough to see that he's taken me into what appears to be a cozy living space—complete with couches and a roaring fireplace.

At first, I assume he's going to lay me down on the coach, but instead he makes a beeline for the plush rug in front of the fireplace, laying me down gently but then grabbing my wrists in his hands and pinning them above my head. I lie there like that, my legs spread wide, still wrapped around his waist, staring up at him.

"Don't ever toy with my heart again, Emma," he says, his voice hard—but I can hear the plea within it. "I wouldn't survive it."

"I won't," I breathe, and I mean it. With every fiber of my being, I mean it. "I'm yours, Ezra. All of me."

His eyes darken, and he presses his arousal against me. He works his jaw, staring down at me with a desire I never thought possible. "Naked," he demands. "Now."

He releases my wrists long enough for me to pull my t-shirt up over my head; then reach behind my back, unclasping my bra.

I fiddle with my jeans, and once I've unbuttoned them, Ezra leans back, grabs the waistband, and slides them off of me. He does the same with my panties, leaving me completely nude in the glow of the fireplace.

He pins me back down with one hand holding both wrists above my head, and I pant, staring up at him, waiting for his next move. He lazily draws his finger along my skin, sliding along my stomach, making circles on my breast, around my nipple.

He leans down to press his lips against my ear. "Sweetheart, should I punish you for being so bad?" he whispers.

My heartbeat stutters. "Punish?" I repeat, equal parts fear and arousal coursing through me.

"I have half a mind to tie you up and torture you until you're begging for release," he murmurs.

My core tightens, and I roll my eyes back. *Fuck.* My breath is coming out in ragged gasps. "Whatever you think I deserve … Mr. Bishop."

"Fuck," he groans against my neck, digging his fingers into the flesh of my breast.

He sits up suddenly, yanking me after him. He stands, leading me over to the couch where he sits and then pulls me over his lap so that my ass is in the air. I yelp quietly in surprise, but that yelp is replaced by a moan when he begins sliding his finger slowly along my slit.

I steady myself against the couch cushions, spreading my legs so he has better access.

"You like being bent over my knee like a bad girl?" he teases.

I bite my lip. To my utter shock, I do. I nod, but Ezra isn't taking that.

"Do you?" he asks again, slipping a finger inside of me.

I gasp. "Yes," I pant. "Yes, yes."

I hear him chuckle, and he beings slowly thrusting that finger in and out of me. I moan, arching my back, pushing back against his hand, desperate for more.

He suddenly pulls his finger out of me, replacing it with a gentle yet firm slap across my ass. I shriek, more so in shock than from pain.

I feel Ezra lean down toward my ear. "Be a good girl and take what I give you," he murmurs.

"Yes, Mr. Bishop," I breathe.

I can feel his cock twitching beneath my belly at my use of his last name. I smirk, feeling all the more aroused knowing how much he likes that.

He inserts his finger back inside me, quickly adding a second to the mix, and soon I'm a whimpering mess while Ezra fingerfucks me to his heart's content. I can feel my orgasm building, and I know Ezra can feel it too, because he roughly pulls out of me just before I tumble over the edge.

I whimper in frustration but resign myself to my fate. It's torture, but I'm loving every second of it.

He starts again, working me up, up, up until I'm almost there, and then snatching my release away with a satisfied smirk. He does it again. And again. And again. Until I'm writhing on his lap, crying, begging, unable to think of anything other than him, him, him.

"*Ezra*," I whimper.

"How long do you think you can take it, sweetheart?" he asks me.

I grip the couch, summoning every ounce of strength I have. "As long as you … need me to," I stutter.

He caresses my clit, murmuring in approval. "That's my good girl."

He shifts, urging me to get up. I do, on wobbly legs. He stands, pointing to the floor. "On your hands and knees," he instructs.

I do as he says, any semblance of dignity gone. At this point, I'll do anything and everything for this man. Whatever he wants.

He slides down his sweatpants, revealing his hard cock. I feel him moving up behind me, and I then I feel the tip of him at my entrance. I moan in anticipation, sure I'll come from just the feel of him inside of me.

He grips my hips, readying himself, and then he slowly slides the length of him inside of me. I gasp as he stretches my walls, splitting me open in the most delicious way possible. But he's not gentle for long.

He immediately starts thrusting, jostling my body as he fucks me. He reaches for my hair at the base of my neck, pulling my head back as he pumps into me. I gasp and moan, submitting my body to him.

"You promise to be my good girl from now on?" he asks between thrusts.

"Yes," I pant, the pressure within my core rising and rising. "I promise."

"You're *mine*," he growls. "Mine to love, mine to protect," he thrusts into me—hard, "and mine to fuck."

I cry out as my orgasm crashes through me. My limbs shake, and I lurch forward, my arms no longer able to hold me up. Ezra follows close behind, stilling as he empties himself inside of me.

He pulls out, quickly gathering me up in his arms as the waves of my orgasm continue to wash through me. I cling to him, wrapped against his chest, as I come down from the high, whimpering softly.

He presses a soft kiss to my forehead. "I mean it," he whispers. "You're mine, Emma."

I reach up to gently cup his face.

He smiles. "And I'm yours."

Epilogue

Ezra

One Year Later

"You and your spicy romance novels," I say with a shake of my head.

Emma pushes a strand of her long, red hair out of her face, laughing that melodic laugh of hers. I swear I'll never get enough of it. She peers at me over a pair of bright pink sunglasses, her tan skin practically sparkling in the sunlight. "As if you didn't read this first," she shoots back, repositioning herself in her lounge chair.

I sit up, my toes scrunching in the sand beneath us as I lean toward her, taking a closer look. The sound of ocean waves thirty feet away caresses my ears. "Oh yeah, I might have already read that one," I say with a shrug.

She cackles in triumph, slapping me lightly with the book. I glance back over my shoulder at the Bar Harbor beach house behind us. The beach house that, almost exactly a year ago, we'd basically started our relationship in.

I think back on the last year. The ups and down, everything that led us here. Other than our rocky start, it's been a fairytale. Something for those romance books Emma loves so much and I pretend to hate.

The buzz around Diane's and my divorce died down within a week or two. I guess normal people don't really care all that much about local celebrity drama. Can't say I blame them. Diane and I divorced somewhat amicably—as amicably as two people can, I think. She's set for life—without it truly impacting me at all—and is off living somewhere in Italy with her new lover. Whatever. I hope she's happy, although I don't spend much time thinking about it.

Justin, thankfully, never showed his ugly face again. Neither I, nor Emma, have heard from him. Hopefully he's learned from his mistakes and become a better person. Who knows? And if that video ever shows up somewhere, I'll keep true to that promise to sue him into the ground.

I glance at the time on my watch, glancing around. "We should head inside," I suggest.

Emma gives me a curious look. "Why? It's so nice out."

"I don't know, I …" I purse my lips. "I'm getting kind of cold."

She squints up at the hot sun beating down on us. "You can head in, I might stay out for a little longer."

"I'm afraid I'll miss you too much," I insist.

She laughs.

I stand. "Come on, I'll make us some lattes." I'm hoping that will coax her. There's an expensive espresso machine in the kitchen that she loves.

She still seems a little bewildered by my request, but she acquiesces, slipping her sandals on and following me the few steps to our porch and then into the house.

Once inside, I shoot off a text with my phone, then make sure she's in the kitchen with me while I make the espresso.

"Cinnamon?" I ask.

"Of course," she replies, smoothing out the wrinkles in her sun dress.

I glance out the window while preparing the drinks. You can't quite see much except the space directly in front of our house—much to my luck. I glance at Emma, then focus back on the coffees.

I purposefully take my time, presenting her with her latte with a dash of cinnamon on top.

She thanks me with a smile, immediately bringing it to her lips and sipping. "What if we go out on the boat this afternoon?" she asks.

I shrug, pretending to ponder the idea. "Maybe," I say. I have a sailboat docked at the Bar Harbor marina, and Emma has finally gotten enough of a knack for it to help me take it out.

She frowns. "Not feeling up to it today?" she guesses.

I shrug again, nonchalantly checking my phone. "Just kinda tired," I say.

She nods in acceptance, taking a seat at the dining room table. I glance past her, out the window to the beach, even though I know I won't see much. I check my phone again, and my eyes light up. A text from my assistant.

Everything's ready.

I straighten my shirt—a nice, short-sleeved button up—and swallow. I pat my pants pocket, feeling the outline of a small box. Damn, I didn't think I'd be nervous for this. I really didn't.

I turn to Emma, holding out a hand. "Come with me," I request with a smile.

She smiles back, but her brows furrow in slight confusion. I motion for her to leave her coffee, and then I lead her to the back door, stepping out into the soft sunlight. "We were just outside," she says with a laugh.

I don't reply, simply grasp her hand tighter as I pull her down the steps to the beach. The lounge chairs we'd been sitting in barely ten minutes ago are gone, leaving a straight path through the sand. Once on the beach, I turn right, and that's when Emma sees it.

She gasps, putting her free hand over her mouth. Her eyes meet mine, already teary, and fuck am I going to have a hard time keeping it together.

Just twenty feet away, nestled in the sandy beach, is an array of flowers. Rose petals lead the way, scattered in the sand, to the outline of a heart made by bouquets of flowers. Behind it is a floral arrangement, standing upright, arranged in boxed letters that spell out the words, "Marry Me?"

My heart beating in my ears, I lead Emma through the rose petals to stand in the center of the heart. By the time I turn to her, tears are already making their way down her cheeks.

I chuckle softly, reaching out to gently brush some of the tears away with my thumb. "Sweetheart," I begin, and it only makes her tears come faster. "I love you more than I even thought possible."

She grasps my hand in hers, pulling it tightly against her chest.

"I know it's only been a year, but I can't stand the thought of you ever not being mine. When my life felt like it was on the brink of falling apart, you saved me. You're my light, my love, my everything."

I pull my hand from her grasp, sinking to a knee before her and pulling the ring box from my pocket. "Emma Hayes," I say, and her eyes sparkle through her tears. "Make me the luckiest man alive and marry me?"

I open the ring box, revealing the Emma ring—the one she'd picked out a year ago to add to our store, the one she'd said she would've chosen for herself, the ring that has reminded me of her every day since.

Recognition dawns on her face, and then in answer to my question, she nods furiously. "Yes," she cries through choked emotion. "Yes, Ezra, yes."

I place the ring on her shaky finger before she reaches for me, and I stumble to my feet, pulling her against me for a kiss. She clings to my shirt, pulling me closer. I smile against her lips—our first kiss as fiancés.

She pulls back, glancing around at the bouquets and flower arrangements. "How did you do this?" she laughs.

"My assistant," I say with a smile.

She nods knowingly.

"My assistant," I say, leaning down to graze the nape of her neck with my lips, "who is no longer here."

She giggles, catching on and playfully swatting my shoulder. "Lead the way, Mr. Bishop."

I growl, leaning down to scoop her up into my arms. "I love when you call me that," I murmur, turning on my heel and stalking across the sand toward the house.

She leans her head against my shoulder. "I know."

I push open the back door, stalking into the house and setting her down. "And soon," I say, moving to pin her against the wall, "I'll get to call you Mrs. Bishop."

She grabs the collar of my shirt, pulling me in for a kiss.

Penelope Ryan

Penelope Ryan writes sizzling hot romances with dominant men and lots of dirty talk and spice. When she isn't writing, she's cuddling with her cat, crafting fancy cinnamon lattes, and ready lots and lots of smutty romance novels.

Other books by Penelope Ryan:

The Billionaire's Obsession

The Billionaire's Wife

My Best Friend's Billionaire Brother

Tempting the Billionaire

Teacher's Pet

Losing It

The Arrangement

Small Town Billionaire

Want a free digital copy of *Losing It*? Go to:

penelope-ryan-books.com

and click "Free Book!" at the top to download your copy.

Hi!

Did you enjoy the book?

Authors and readers depend on reviews. If you enjoyed the book, please consider leaving a review. Thank you so much!

Made in the USA
Las Vegas, NV
24 December 2024

15246717R00079